LET SLIP

The two dogs walloped into each other not more than five feet from Didi. They were soon joined in combat.

The fight ended quickly, however, before it ever got going.

A terrible sound splintered the morning air.

There was a *crack!* And then an echo.

The dogs stopped scrapping immediately. Every living thing—human and beast—froze in place.

This was hunting country. Everyone in Lubin's Field knew the sound of a high-powered bullet fired at close range in clear weather.

Didi looked up at the makeshift stage. The poet was standing. The ministers were standing. The mayor was standing.

Only John Breitland was down—his brains blown out.

Dr. Nightingale Rides to the Hounds

A DEIRDRE QUINN
NIGHTINGALE
MYSTERY

Lydia Adamson

A SIGNET BOOK

SIGNET
Published by the Penguin Group
Penguin Books USA Inc., 375 Hudson Street,
New York, New York 10014, U.S.A.
Penguin Books Ltd, 27 Wrights Lane,
London W8 5TZ, England
Penguin Books Australia Ltd,
Ringwood, Victoria, Australia
Penguin Books Canada Ltd, 10 Alcorn Avenue,
Toronto, Ontario, Canada M4V 3B2
Penguin Books (N.Z.) Ltd, 182–190 Wairau Road,
Auckland 10, New Zealand

Penguin Books Ltd, Registered Offices:
Harmondsworth, Middlesex, England

First published by Signet, an imprint of Dutton Signet,
a division of Penguin Books USA Inc.

First Printing, February, 1997
10 9 8 7 6 5 4 3 2 1

PUBLISHER'S NOTE
This is a work of fiction. Names, characters, places, and incidents
either are the product of the author's imagination or are used
fictitiously, and any resemblance to actual persons, living or
dead, events, or locales is entirely coincidental.

Chapter 1

It was only a mile and a half from Deirdre Quinn Nightingale's property to the abandoned piece of land called Lubin's Field.

It took the procession a full hour to make the trip.

And what a strange procession it was on that late Sunday morning, one week after Easter.

At the front of the column, like General Sheridan, Deirdre Quinn Nightingale, DVM, rode her horse at a stately pace.

Stretched out behind her were all her troops—better known as her "elves," as she called them; the permanent residents she had inherited from her mother along with the land and the house.

Behind Didi and her fine horse Promise Me, walked elf number one: old Charlie Gravis, her veterinary assistant. He was leading Sara, a Spotted Poland China sow.

Then came the acerbic Mrs. Tunney, the "housekeeper" of the Nightingale home. She carried two of Sara's piglets in a large wicker basket.

After Mrs. Tunney came young Trent Tucker, driving his battered pickup truck at a snail's pace.

And in the open back of the truck sat Abigail with four of the yard dogs—four being as many as she had been able to round up. The numberless barn cats had eluded her altogether. She had failed to corral even one of them.

The dogs howled and moaned and never gave up trying to jump out of the truck bed. But Abigail patrolled the perimeter resolutely, gently pulling them away from the edge.

Didi was not enjoying herself. She found the whole thing rather ridiculous.

The procession was going to Lubin's Field because that was where the blessings of the animals would take place. The ritual was cosponsored by two churches in Hillsbrook, neither of which Didi—nor any of her elves—belonged to.

Anybody who had a farm animal or a pet was urged to bring it to Lubin's Field, where the ministers would bless the dear beasts en masse.

This was the second such festival in Hillsbrook. It was patterned on the justly famous annual rite at the Church of St. John the Divine, in New York City, which even attracted elephants.

Didi had ignored requests by Mrs. Tunney

and Abigail last year, but this year the two of them had been so persistent they wore her down.

In a moment of weakness, she had agreed.

And here she was. Unhappy. Feeling foolish. To her mind the creatures of the earth are born "blessed." Additional ministrations are unnecessary. Even excessive.

The moment the field was visible, Didi climbed down from her horse and held the reins in her hand tightly.

Promise Me was a bit frightened, she could tell.

The field was literally a carpet of beasts and their proud owners.

There were goats, sheep, calves, work horses and riding horses, dogs and cats without number, birds in cages and parrots on shoulders. There were many exotic beasts also: from boas to llamas to glass-encased scorpions.

And there were children . . . so many children. Enough for a new-style, sneaker-wearing Crusade.

The dairy farmers had obviously taken a pass on the festival. Only five or six dairy cows were present, placidly looking over the throng, oblivious to the fretting babies and the general cacophony. As Didi had noted so many times in the past, dairy cows, for whatever reason, were virtually fearless.

A sturdy wooden stand had been constructed in the center of the field—the altar—and the structure was ringed with sound equipment.

Didi could see Father Jessup and Reverend Arlo already on the stage.

Also on stage was John Breitland, head of the Hillsbrook chapter of the Dutchess County Animal Welfare League.

Breitland was the last surviving member of the once-wealthy and socially prominent Breitland family, manufacturers of dairy equipment.

Their company had gone bankrupt in 1973. There was nothing left of the Breitland fortune but a large house and 2,100 of the most beautiful acres in Hillsbrook. John Breitland lived in that house alone. He was only forty-one years old, but he was treated with the kind of deference accorded to a powerful patriarch. Even those neighbors who had known him all his life called him Mr. Breitland—the influence and prestige of the family name still being strong.

Didi guided her contingent to an empty space left of the portable stage.

Practically all the assembled were neighbors and friends and business acquaintances. Everybody seemed to know everybody and there was much nodding and waving in greeting. There was little conversation, however, because the animals to be blessed had to be watched and controlled.

One slipup, and a chain reaction could turn Lubin's Field into a land of chaos. One dog could nip one horse who would then kick out at one cat who would dart away and scratch the nose of one sow while fleeing—and, well, the possibilities were endless.

Didi drove a sharp wooden stake into the ground and tethered Promise Me to it.

Trent Tucker parked the truck perpendicular to the horse and Charlie then tied the big sow to a wheel axle with a frayed rope.

Mrs. Tunney deposited the piglets beside her.

Abigail stayed in the open back of the truck, tending the yard dogs, who now were greedily surveying the other dogs in the field as if they couldn't decide who to attack first.

"Look! The mayor!" Mrs. Tunney called out in a hoarse stage whisper.

Sure enough, Lilly Caro, the mayor of Hillsbrook, was walking swiftly toward the wooden stage.

She was a tall woman with bristling gray hair that stood up all around her head like a cactus. She always wore farm work clothes and carried a clipboard.

Her husband had started the first successful bakery in the Hillsbrook area. When he ran off with a young stable girl Lilly had shut down the bakery and gone into politics. There were rumors that she was about to seek state office.

"If she's going to bless our pigs," Charlie said, "we might as well turn them into pork chops now."

"That is a terrible thing to say," Mrs. Tunney chastised. "She is the best mayor this town has ever had."

"And I'm Winston Churchill," Charlie retorted.

"At least she cleaned out the crooks."

"What crooks? She's been in office for two years. She found one pathetic character who bribed somebody on the zoning commission. And it may not even have been a bribe."

"Face it, Charlie Gravis. You can't stand the idea of a lady mayor."

"I don't like a blind lady mayor."

"You don't have to see in this town. All you have to do is smell."

Didi saw a political battle royale brewing, so she stepped right into the breech. "Did you bring that thermos, Mrs. Tunney?"

Before Didi could get her answer, applause erupted behind her, drowning out Mrs. Tunney's response.

It was Burt Conyers striding through the crowd.

The applause was a bit ironic and a bit derisive. Conyers was a certified eccentric. He went about in all seasons in the same sheepskin vest and sneakers and bamboo cane.

He had always proclaimed himself a poet, but no one in Hillsbrook believed him until an Albany public television station did a program on him and declared him to be an important rural poet in the Robert Frost tradition.

Since then, as a local literary celebrity, he was always invited to invocations and convocations to open the ceremonies with a poem.

As for the poetry itself, it had a macabre pastoral bent. His work was usually about roadkill or diseased trees or rutting deer or mushrooms as phallic images.

The moment the poet reached the wooden platform and negotiated the steps up to the stage, Mayor Caro walked to the pulpit.

Didi rubbed Promise Me's nose. The big horse had settled in quite happily.

Didi felt a tug on her sleeve. It was Mrs. Tunney handing her the thermos. She unscrewed the top, poured some tea into the cup, and drank. It was good. Lots of honey and lemon.

What a glorious day it is, Didi thought, looking at the bright blue sky with a single swath of clouds and the woods past the field.

She rescrewed the top and handed the thermos back to Mrs. Tunney.

Mayor Caro's speech was short, sweet, and nonpolitical. She simply welcomed the people and the animals, then sat down on one of the folding metal chairs arrayed on stage.

The poet approached the pulpit.

Didi's cynicism was beginning to vanish altogether. She was beginning to feel a sense of strong community with all her Hillsbrook neighbors and their beasts in that field. She was beginning, in fact, to feel elated.

But where was her good friend Rose Vigdor? she suddenly thought.

Didi looked around. Ah! Rose and her three dogs were about a hundred yards away.

Rose was lying blissfully on her back. Huck, the Corgi, was chewing happily on one corner of the blanket. The two German shepherds, Aretha and Bozo, were sitting alertly, side by side, watching the stage, obviously waiting anxiously for the blessing, or perhaps a dog bone.

Didi lay her head against Promise Me's neck. For all she knew, her horse, too, was anxious to be blessed. One thing Didi had learned as a vet was that the mind of a horse is bewildering and unfathomable.

Burt Conyers started to recite his poem. He fairly shouted it, reading from a single sheet of paper that he had smoothed out on the pulpit.

> Behold the wildflowers
> Those sweet carpets of death.
> Suck in their sweet strychnine
> pollen!

On my! Didi thought. He's not going to lighten up, even this morning.

She tuned him out and stared at the sky instead. A V formation of geese was moving very high and very fast. Going home.

Suddenly Didi had one of those strange intuitions: she was being watched . . . stared at.

It was a very strong intuition.

Slowly she turned her head.

She found the source, and groaned.

It was Carswell, the beagle. He was standing about twenty yards from her—staring. Ears up. Tail up.

She looked around desperately for Mrs. Niles, his owner. But she was nowhere to be seen.

Carswell had never forgiven Dr. Nightingale.

About a year ago he had chased some critter through barbed wire and cut himself badly. The wounds had become infected. Didi had treated the beagle successfully, but for some reason the local freezing agent she had used as an anesthetic had not worked very well. Carswell blamed her for his suffering, as well he might, although he had got into his own trouble. He would set upon her or her red jeep anytime he caught sight of them—anywhere. Two of the attacks occurred in town, one in the cleaning store.

There was no time now to plan an escape.

The beagle launched his attack with a barely audible yip and ran toward her, low to the ground.

Sweet Abigail of the golden tresses, or dim-witted Abigail, as some people called her behind her back, saw the charge and released one of the yard dogs, nicknamed Ironhead, to blunt the attack.

The two dogs walloped into each other not more than five feet from Didi. They were soon joined in combat.

The fight ended quickly, however. Before it ever really got going.

A terrible sound splintered the morning air.

There was a *crack!* And then an echo.

The dogs stopped scrapping immediately. Every living thing—human and beast—froze in place.

This was hunting country. Everyone in Lubin's Field knew the sound of a high-powered bullet fired at close range. In clear weather.

Didi looked up at the makeshift wooden stage.

The poet was standing. The ministers were standing. The mayor was standing.

Only John Breitland was lying on the wooden planks.

The bullet had entered his right eye and blown his brains out onto Father Jessup.

Eyes bulging, Father Jessup remained as he had been, a cry caught in his throat.

Burt Conyers decided to finish his poem. But the unblessed beasts and their protectors were already fleeing Lubin's Field.

Chapter 2

Officer Wynton Chung pulled the police crusier off the road and shut the engine. Next to him sat Allie Voegler, the only detective in the Hillsbrook Police Department.

"We've probably been here twenty times in the last ten days," Chung noted testily.

"What else do you have to do?" Allie retorted and climbed out of the vehicle.

He stared across the road to Lubin's Field. This was where the shooter had parked his pickup. Then he had rested his handgun on the fender, placed a scope on top of the long .44-caliber barrel, and blown John Breitland away. At least this was the best scenario the Hillsbrook police, in consultation with the state police labs, could come up with. Further ballistic evidence would not be forthcoming—the bullet had shattered and only fragments found; no shell casings had been left at the scene.

"You're not going to find anything, Allie. We went over this place with a vacuum cleaner. Besides, everyone knows who the shooter was."

"You mean Orin Rafael?"

"Hell, yes. We have a dozen witnesses who heard him threaten Breitland in the diner. And we got motive. Breitland shut Rafael's boarding stable down. He put the poor bastard out of business."

"Breitland didn't shut the boarding stable, Officer Chung. The Animal Welfare League did."

"But Breitland was head of the league. He's the one who got the court order."

"No. The league's attorneys got a court order. Based on the fact that three horses died in that stable."

"You're splitting hairs, Allie."

"Maybe. But Orin doesn't know guns. I don't think he ever fired one. Our shooter probably used one of those sophisticated new handgun systems—with interchangeable barrels and scopes. And even more important, Orin Rafael has a very good alibi."

"He was checked into a New York City hotel."

"Exactly."

"Come on. Anyone can set up something like that. Pay a guy to check in under his name. It happens all the time."

Voegler didn't reply. He stared at the ground.

"Did you know Breitland, Allie?"

"Not really. I mean, I met him three or four times. We moved in different circles."

"The guy intrigues me."

"He's dead."

"Yeah, I know. But he still intrigues me. For example, he was one of the big shots in that fox hunting nonsense. Before it closed down."

"You mean the Hillsbrook Hunt?"

"Sure. That's it. I heard about it. I heard it was hunt breakfasts and tally ho and packs of hounds and horns and masters of the hunt and whipper-ins—and whipper-outs—if there is any such thing. Oh, and don't forget the silver brandy flasks. You know what I'm talking about: red caps and riding crops. The whole nine yards."

"That's the way it was," Allie agreed.

"Well, answer me this. How could a guy who used to hunt foxes for sport end up as the president of the Dutchess County Animal Welfare League?"

"Why not? I hunt deer and I'm a member of the Animal Welfare League. At least I send them twenty-five dollars a year."

"But you're crazy, Allie," Chung said, and then started to laugh uproariously at his own joke.

"Why don't we get to work," Allie suggested angrily.

Chung got out of the car.

"You're going to look at those tire treads again?" he asked in disbelief.

"That's right," Allie affirmed.

They walked to the tracks, about ten yards off the road. The furrows were still clearly visible.

"Okay. Now hear me out. I've been thinking," Allie said. "We know what the shooter did. He drove off the road and then ran the pickup back and forth over his tracks to obscure them."

"Right. And he did a helluva good job."

"But why?"

"So we couldn't lift a tire track."

"But, Chung, listen. Everyone uses all-weather year-around radials on pickup trucks now. Maybe two or three brands are sold in this area. Tire tracks wouldn't mean a damn thing here. Even if we could lift a track, it'd fit about ten thousand vehicles with the same tires in a hundred-mile radius."

"You got a point."

"So why did he try to obscure those tire tracks?"

"You got me."

"Maybe because he had old-fashioned snow tires on the pickup. Maybe he hadn't changed them yet. And old-fashioned snow tires, specially with studs, leave big marks—and not too many people use them anymore."

Chung squatted down and stared at the

tracks, nodding his head approvingly at Allie's theory.

"You know, boss, you ain't as dumb as they say you are. I'm going to write a letter to that chick you've been trying to jump into bed with. I'm going to tell her what she's missing."

Allie lashed out with his foot, knocking the younger cop over.

"Don't ever call Didi Nightingale a chick," he warned.

Deirdre Quinn Nightingale, doctor of veterinary medicine, strode into the barn, followed by a puffing Charlie Gravis.

She had developed this aggressive way of making an entrance when on rounds as a kind of defense. When she first came back to Hillsbrook to practice, many of her clients simply couldn't take her seriously as a veterinarian because they had known her as a child.

But there was no client to impress here. The barn that morning appeared empty except for Glowworm, the big chestnut mare standing quietly in her stall.

"Mrs. Donniger!" Didi called out.

There was no answer.

"They beg you to get here fast. Then they're nowhere to be found," Charlie complained.

Didi ignored him. "Mrs. Donniger," she called again.

This time a figure appeared at the far end of the barn and started to hobble toward them.

"She looks like she got hit by a tractor," Charlie whispered as the woman came close.

The formerly robust sixty-year-old widow Donniger had obviously run into some serious difficulty. One wrist was in a cast. She was using a cane with the other hand, and the right side of her face was black and blue.

"Aren't I a mess?" Lilly Donniger declared when she had positioned herself in front of Didi.

"What happened?" asked Didi.

"Glowworm threw me. And then stepped on me! Oh, she was a naughty girl. But there must be something wrong with her to do such a bad thing. Very wrong."

"When did this happen?" Didi took her eyes away from Mrs. Donniger and began to edge closer to the mare in her stall.

"Yesterday morning. I took her out for her morning ride. As always. And then suddenly— we weren't even through the gate yet—she wheeled and reared a bit and I went flying off. This has never happened before. Never."

"Maybe she was spooked by something," Charlie offered. "Could have been a rabbit."

"Nothing spooked her," Lilly replied. "Glowworm doesn't spook. No. Something's bothering her."

"How long have you had Glowworm, Lilly?" Didi asked.

"Five or six years."

"How old is she now?"

"About thirteen."

"Have you taken her out of the stall since the accident?"

"No."

Charlie asked, "You want me to jog her in the aisle?" He was proud that as his age he could still jog a horse.

"Not yet," Didi told him. Then she walked to the stall, opened the latch, and walked inside. Glowworm snorted and turned to greet the visitor.

"What a beautiful lady you are," murmured Didi. She immediately picked up on the fact that the mare was in some sort of discomfort. She moved too delicately, like she was afraid to break eggs that had been placed beneath her hooves. But there were no eggs.

Didi reached into her pants pocket and pulled out a small lump of brown sugar. Holding it in her palm, she offered it to the mare. Glowworm accepted happily, slopping saliva all over Didi's hand.

Didi gave her another lump, then stepped away to look down at the mare's line.

"Get the halter, Charlie. I'll examine her in the aisle."

About five seconds later she said, "Hold up, Charlie."

She had seen something on the horse's back—a bulge of sorts, near the front part of the group.

Didi gave Glowworm another piece of sugar, then, starting with a caress of the mare's graceful neck, ran her hand gently and expertly down the length of the horse's backbone.

Glowworm edged away. She gave a warning snort. Didi dropped her hand.

"Where did you get Glowworm?" she asked Mrs. Donniger.

"From the Hillsbrook Hunt Club. When they disbanded, a lot of hunters were for sale. And Glowworm was one of the best."

Didi smiled. Yes. It all made sense now. "Can you come into the stall for a minute, Mrs. Donniger?"

The wounded woman limped into the stall.

"Do you see that?" Didi asked, pointing at the mare's back.

"What?"

"That protuberance."

"Yes, I see it now."

"That's why she threw you. It was nothing personal. Just a luxation of the sacroiliac joint."

Lilly Donniger looked stupefied.

Using her hands to illustrate the skeletal structure of a horse, Didi explained: "The sacroiliac joint is the only articulation between the backbone and the pelvis. When a horse takes off wrong or lands wrong on a jump . . . when the back leg is too far forward, for example . . . that causes the two halves of the joint to rotate in opposite directions. Which then causes a tear of the ligaments on the front of the joint . . . which then allows the pelvis to move up and forward . . . Voila! What you see."

"Oh my poor Glowworm," moaned Mrs. Donniger.

Didi realized her semitechnical explanation had produced the wrong response entirely.

"No, no, Mrs. Donniger. What I'm trying to tell you is that it's not serious. It's quite common. It's called Hunter Bump because so many hunters and jumpers get it."

"But I don't take her over fences," the older woman protested.

"I know that. But that was the way she got the condition originally. Now, she might have brought back the condition just by taking a misstep or rolling in the stall. There is no real treatment for it but rest. It'll go away. It's not serious."

Charlie, who had been standing silently with the halter, burst out laughing. He just couldn't keep it in. Here was the vet telling Lilly Donniger that the *horse*'s condition wasn't serious. But what about Mrs. Donniger herself? She had required five thousand dollars' worth of medical treatment. Oh, it was funny.

He stifled the laugh when Didi gave him a lethal look. Then he busied himself with the halter, as if he were mending it.

"Rest, Mrs. Donniger. That's all Glowworm needs. Don't ride her. Don't turn her out. If she gets a bit restless just hand walk her in the aisle."

"Thank you! Thank you!" Lilly Donniger seemed to do a little dance with her cane. "Send me your bill. I'll pay it immediately. Send me a bill."

Didi agreed to send the bill promptly. She marched out of the barn and climbed into the red jeep. Charlie took his own sweet time, studying the lay of the Donniger land like the old dairy farmer he was—for drainage, for crops, for nothing at all.

When Charlie finally climbed in beside her, Didi said, "I'm going to the Hillsbrook Diner for some breakfast. You're invited."

"Well, thank you, Miss Quinn, but I ate early and my stomach's a little funny. Could you just drop me in town? I have some errands to do. Then I'll get a lift back to the house."

The entire trip to the village from Donniger's place took about ten minutes. Five minutes into the ride Charlie said, "I once had a sacroiliac condition."

"Did you, Charlie?"

"Oh yes. And I'll tell you—it was painful."

"Was it?" Didi knew something was coming but she didn't know what.

"It was before you came back home to practice . . . before you hung out your shingle— Deirdre Quinn Nightingale, Doctor of Veterinary Medicine."

Didi winced. Whenever Charlie started that shingle nonsense he was going to make some kind of point about the way she conducted herself professionally.

"Anyway, I went to a whole bunch of doctors for this sacroiliac condition of mine. None of them helped me."

"That's sad, Charlie."

"But they all gave me something to take."

"You mean medicine?"

"Yep. Pills. Ointments. All manner of medicine. I told them it didn't work, but they kept on prescribing that stuff for me to take."

"I get your point, Charlie. I get your point!" Didi said angrily. The old man gave her an innocent look. Didi knew, in fact, that he was making a good point. Vets can't survive on fees alone. The bulk of the income has to come from pharmaceuticals. Unlike physicians who utilize drugstores to fill prescriptions, vets are their own pharmacies. It is the profit from pharmaceuticals that determines the financial health of a veterinary practice, particularly in a dairy farming community.

"I could have prescribed a painkiller or a muscle relaxer for that mare. It wouldn't have helped her condition, but it wouldn't have hurt."

Charlie nodded sagely.

"But, Charlie," Didi warned, "you don't know a lot about horses. Milk cows maybe, but not horses."

Charlie pouted a bit.

"Let me explain something. Horses are very strange creatures. When they're hurting a little, they calm down and quiet down. They wait it out. But if you mask their little pains, they revert back to their high-spirited ways and they hurt themselves, sometimes real bad. That's what happens at the racetracks all the time. A trainer has a horse that's stepping a bit gingerly. The trainer freezes the limb and send the horse out to run because he needs the purse money. The horse runs sound for three furlongs and then breaks down. You see what I'm saying, Charlie? Glowworm was not in a whole lot of pain. She'll get better by herself as long as she's not ridden."

"I sure do see," Charlie said and gave her one of his wise looks that said: "You got a house with four people other than yourself to feed . . . a fancy horse . . . dogs, cats, and a whole passel

of pigs . . . a walk-in clinic that's doing badly . . .
three vehicles . . . and back taxes to pay. So you
better start doing what you have to do."

Didi knew the spiel by heart. She turned the
tape deck on—loud.

They sat in the police car, just off the road, and
stared at the shuttered Breitland house.

"It doesn't look like much," Wynton Chung
said. "I mean, it's not the kind of house you
would think a rich family once lived in. It kind
of reminds me of one of those three-story wood
frame boardinghouses you see in the poor section of Kingston."

Allie laughed. "That boardinghouse, as you
call it, is sitting on a couple of million dollars'
worth of land. Go behind the house and walk
north and it'll probably take you three days to
get to the end of the Breitland property."

"So what?"

"So all I'm trying to say is that old Hillsbrook
money bought land; new Hillsbrook money
buys fancy houses. And the Breitlands were
fairly old money."

"Did he live there alone?"

"All alone."

"No girlfriends?"

"Not that we know of. No friends at all. At
least not since the Hillsbrook Hunt shut down.
It was different then. A lot of the members sta-

bled their horses with him, and the dogs were kept there. And the hunt breakfasts were in his house. But that was then. Now he gets all his groceries delivered. He seems to have stayed in the house most of the day listening to opera. Once a week he went to Rhinebeck where the offices of the Animal Welfare League were located. Once a year he went to Europe for a couple of months. France and Italy. Funny, isn't it? The man was born, raised, and murdered in Hillsbrook. And that's all we know about him. Oh yeah . . . we do know that if you invited him to participate in a community event he would accept. We do know that."

"Did he ever work?" Chung asked.

"Not that we could discover. Of course, he didn't have to work. He went to Yale Law School, graduated, passed the New York Bar, but never practiced."

"Who took care of that big house for him?"

"Don't know. There was no housekeeper. He was alone. Even the horses were gone."

"What happened to them?"

"He sold them off after the hunt closed down. And the dogs."

"Why did the hunt club close down, Allie?"

"Lack of contiguous land, I suppose. Too much development. All those horses and hounds probably didn't know what to do when they burst out of the woods after a fox and found themselves in a shopping mall. Jumping cars like they were fences."

"Foxes don't play by the rules," Chung noted.

Allie tapped the dashboard. "Let's go," he said.

"Where?"

"The Ridge."

"What for?"

"To see a man about a pickup truck."

Chung started the engine and they headed into the hilly section north and west of the village called the Ridge. It was where the Hillsbrook poor lived—in trailers, without, for the most part, electricity or running water—except for those few who had their own generators.

Allie gave Chung the directions. They were complex. Officer Chung had to turn suddenly on roads that were very narrow and watch out for abandoned vehicles or illegal garbage dumps. The Ridge was truly grimy and dangerous for the casual motorist.

Finally Chung gunned the big car up a steep hillock and it came to rest on a broad flat stretch of land—a kind of mini plateau that was festooned like a junkyard.

An old-fashioned U.S. Army mess tent was set up amidst two-dozen derelict and stripped vehicles and appliances. The front of the tent was criss-crossed with clotheslines.

Voegler and Chung got out of the vehicle. A

young man was walking toward them. He was very tall and lanky with tattoos up and down both arms.

"Looks like a biker," Chung noted.

"He's just a fool," Allie replied.

The young man stopped, grinned at the visitors, lit a cigarette, and ran one hand through his long dirty blond hair.

"I don't like getting woken at this hour," he said. His voice was oddly mellifluous, given his appearance.

"Too bad," Allie replied, then turned to Wynton and said in a loud voice, "This is Sonny James. He and I have had some problems in the past." Allie turned back to Sonny before continuing. "But that's all over . . . isn't it, Sonny?"

"It was a misunderstanding," Sonny said, falsely accommodating. "Everyone interprets the law differently."

"He's a philosopher," Allie muttered to Chung.

"But I'm glad you came, Detective Voegler. In fact, I was going to pay you a visit in town today."

"Is that so?"

"Yes. I was going to explain to you why I had to blow John Breitland's brains out. But I was confident you'd understand. I mean, old John owed me a lot of money and just wouldn't pay."

Sonny James soaked in the astonished response for a moment and then burst out laughing at his elaborate joke. He pointed a mocking finger at Allie Voegler. "Admit it. You bought it for a minute. You bought it lock, stock, and barrel. You really thought Breitland owed *me* money."

Allie waited until the young man had recovered from the success of his momentary hoodwinking.

"I'd like to take a look at your pickup, Sonny."

"It's not for sale."

"Where is it?"

"On the other side."

"Let's go."

Sonny James led the two officers around the back of the tent and through a maze of dead machines. Allie could hear other voices from within the tent but could see only their shadows.

"Here she is," Sonny said, stopping in front of a freshly painted Toyota pickup. It was about twelve years old and ugly as sin.

Allie broke into a big smile. "Well, look at this," he said. "You got brand new tires on this truck. Isn't that interesting?"

"What's interesting about it?" Sonny demanded.

"Just interesting. Even my partner will find it interesting. A whole bunch of people may find it interesting." He looked at Chung. "Am I overstating the case, Officer? Don't you find it interesting?"

"Sure do," Chung replied.

Allie ran his hand over the tread of the right front radial.

"When did you put them on, Sonny?"

"Few days ago."

"What kind of tires you have on before?"

"Old tires."

"Snow tires?"

"Don't remember."

"With studs?"

"Don't remember."

"Where are they?"

"Burned them."

"Why would you go and do something like that, Sonny? You could sell them. And they make a stink when they burn."

Sonny James didn't answer. Allie said quietly, "Maybe you did shoot John Breitland."

Sonny spat and lit a cigarette. The bicep on his right arm went into a kind of spasm, flexing and unflexing the name Mary, which was tattooed there.

"You have any weapons in the tent, Sonny?"

"Sure."

"What kind?"

"And old shotgun and a new deer rifle."

"What about side arms?"

"No."

"What about one of those high-powered new hunting side arms with a whole mess of interchangeable barrels?"

"No."

"You mind if I look around?"

"Yes, I mind. You want to search my place, you get a warrant."

"Do you know Orin Rafael?"

"Sounds like a dry cereal," Sonny replied.

"Do you know him?"

"No. Never met a man with a name like that."

Allie smiled and stared hard at Sonny James. James stared back and blew cigarette smoke. Chung started to walk back to the car. Then Allie followed.

Sometimes, Charlie thought, Deirdre Quinn Nightingale is so gullible it's unbelievable. She really believed that he wasn't hungry and had errands in town.

I'm always hungry. Everybody knows that, Charlie thought, chuckling to himself.

And the only errand he had to run was—after a seven-year hiatus—to visit his old poker game again. Seven long years.

Charlie peered through the bank window and then quickly turned the corner and hurried along the building line until he came to a small store set way back from the street. A sign over the store read: SHOES—SALES/REPAIRS.

Charlie knocked once, opened the door, and walked into the longest running poker game in Dutchess County and maybe the nation.

It was the dairy farmers' thing. When they finished a rough morning; when they needed a little pleasure; when they wanted the company of like-minded folks, there was always the poker game at the saddle place. It went seven days a week, just like cows had to be milked seven days a week—from ten in the morning till two in the afternoon.

Charlie had once been a fervent member of the game. But he had abandoned it when his finances became too bad; when he became what he was now—an ex dairy farmer who worked as a vet's assistant in exchange for room and board, just like the other people at the Nightingale house worked: Mrs. Tunney, Abigail, and Trent Tucker. Nobody besides the boss lady, Miss Quinn herself, had any cash. And she didn't spread it around to any of the elves, as she referred to Charlie and the others.

The minute he stepped through the door, old Bruce Rexall, the saddler, bounded up from the table, if one could say a spry seventy-six-year-old still bounded.

"Charlie Gravis! I'll be a monkey's uncle. We thought you had died and gone to Arizona."

They made room for Charlie. He played two hands and then began to feel uncomfortable, even though he had won one of the hands by drawing one card to a full house.

The problem was . . . he really didn't know the other players. Oh, he had seen them all in one place or another over the years—in church or in the general store or this or that tavern. But they surely weren't the dairy farmers who used to sit around the table. None of them had those telltale dairyman's hands crisscrossed with fungal growth from years of sticking them into damp muck.

Charlie excused himself and motioned to Bruce Rexall that he wanted to speak to him outside. One of the players said, "Pot too steep for you, old man?"

Charlie ignored him. When he and Rexall were safely outdoors, he asked, "Where are the regulars?"

"What regulars?" Rexall asked.

"The ones who used to play here."

"Most of them are dead, Charlie. What's the matter with you? We're at that age."

"But I know Ike Badian's alive. Where's Ike?" Badian was an old friend of Charlie's. They had drifted apart for no reason whatever. Charlie had not only liked Ike, he had respected him, was even a little jealous of him—in the best sense.

Isaac Badian was a real survivor. He still ran a working dairy herd. Not too big, not too profitable, but he kept on going.

"Ike still comes here often," Rexall said, "but he hasn't been around for the last week or so. He's having some problems."

"What? Is he sick? He can't be as sick as John Breitland. Now, that's sick! Breitland is dead."

Rexall didn't appreciate Charlie's quip. He made a disapproving face. Charlie felt stupid for having made it. The card game had scrambled his brains. Or maybe drawing one card to a full house had unhinged him.

"No," Bruce Rexall answered. "He's not sick. But he did say something about contamination."

"What does that mean? What kind of contamination is he talking about?"

"How should I know? Calm down, Charlie. You're getting all worked up. How about a drink to settle your old nerves? We have a bottle inside."

Charlie suddenly realized that the real reason he had gone to the poker game was simply to see old friends. To talk. To reminisce. And right now he wanted very badly to see Isaac Badian. And he wanted to be standing in a working cow barn. He wanted to smell cows. He wanted to feel alive again instead of trailing after a young girl, helping her treat old mares.

Ike's dairy operation may be in big trouble, he reasoned. Maybe that's what "contamination" meant. Big trouble. He could help his old friend. After all, Ike was the kind of dairyman who wouldn't call a vet even if his whole herd collapsed en masse with one synchronized bellow.

"Drive me over there," he said to the saddler.

"Now?" Rexall asked.

"Right now. Please."

"But I'm in a game, Charlie."

"They can play without you for twenty minutes, man. Just drop me at Ike's and you can get right back."

Rexall stared ruefully at Charlie for a long time. But they both knew there was no way he could say no.

Didi sat in a booth and carefully studied the diner's menu, as if it contained some new dishes. Her blue denim "rounds" shirt was still flecked with wisps of hay from Glowworm's stall. She looked younger than her twenty-eight years—small and thin with short black hair, bangs, and pale green eyes.

Over the denim shirt she wore coveralls with crossed straps. On her feet were rubber boots with the tops turned down, ideal for trekking around in the mud. Beside her on the worn leather seat was her hooded sweatshirt; always carried because Dutchess County weather was shifty in springtime.

"Ready?" The waitress had appeared. Didi did not recognize her and the waitress picked up on her puzzlement.

"I'm just filling in this week," she explained.

"Am I too late for the breakfast specials?"

"No."

"Then I'll have the Triple."

The waitress laughed. "Can you refresh my memory on that one? I had to learn sixteen kinds of special."

"One egg, two pancakes, two strips of bacon."

"How do you want it?"

The television over the counter, about twenty feet from Didi's booth, was switched on. The screen focused. A voice began to speak.

"The egg over easy; the bacon crisp."

"Do you want juice? It comes with the special."

"No juice, just coffee."

The waitress flipped her pad over and started to walk away. She stopped suddenly in mid-stride, her face showing absolute rage.

"What's the matter?" Didi asked.

"If I see that videotape again, I'm going to walk out of here!"

Didi looked at the TV set. She winced. Yes, she, too, had seen that videotape a hundred times during the past ten days. Someone there that day had a video camera focused on the poet reciting and the others on the podium listening.

And then John Breitland's head seemed to explode.

The TV stations kept playing the tape over and over again. And they kept using the same script along with it:

How John Breitland was the last of the family that once ran the largest factory ever to exist in the Hillsbrook area. The Breitlands had been a kind of farm implements dynasty.

How this assassination video echoed the films of the Kennedy assassination in Dallas more than thirty years ago.

How the only suspect in the case, Orin Rafael, had been questioned by the police and released.

Yes, Didi and everyone else in Hillsbrook was weary of the tape, but it kept on appearing.

When the food arrived Didi ate quickly, almost surgically. And as she consumed the last forkful, she had to suppress a burst of laughter, because she had suddenly thought of her dear friend Rose Vigdor, who would go pale as death at the sight of such a breakfast. All that sugar and animal fat and cholesterol. Poor Rose would be mute with horror.

Didi pushed the plate away. She wondered how her friend was doing. She hadn't heard from Rose at all during the past week. Yes, that was what she would do right after breakfast. Check up on Rose. Goodness knows, someone had to keep an eye on Rose Vigdor.

A few minutes later Didi stood in Rose's huge unfinished barn, surrounded by three leaping, barking dogs. She greeted each of them—Aretha, Huck, and Bozo—with a good scratch behind the ears.

From high up on the inside scaffolding Rose called out, "Is that you, Night Gown?"

"It's me!" she shouted in reply.

The elves always called her *Miss Quinn*—Didi's mom's maiden name—because they had known her mother but not her father. There was at least some logic in that.

But Rose seemed to have an endless supply of names for Didi: Nightingale, Night Gown, Night Train, Birdy, Doc, Bugs, Quinlan, Girlfriend, Lulabelle . . . on and on. It was just one of the many reasons the people of Hillsbrook thought Rose was around the bend. The fact that Rose had left a high-paying job in Manhattan to live like a "nature girl" in a drafty unfinished barn with no electricity confirmed their belief in her irrationality. That she was tall and beautiful and blond made her even more suspect.

Rose climbed down and immediately put the

tea kettle on a grate of the small potbellied stove.

"Were you worried about me?" she asked. "Because I haven't called?"

"Not really worried. More curious."

"I was in town yesterday. Everybody is still obsessed with what happened to John Breitland."

"Well," Didi replied, "these kinds of things are—well, it's not the kind of thing you forget easily. It takes a while to get over something like that. There were a lot of people in Lubin's Field that morning . . . and a lot of animals. Anything might have happened."

"There was a lot more than people and animals in that field, my girl," said Rose, a note of menace in her voice.

"What do you mean? What else was there?"

Rose gave her a smug look but said no more.

"What? . . . *What*?" Didi demanded. "You're acting awfully weird, Rose. What are you talking about?"

Rose stretched out her own hands and grabbed Didi's. "It was inevitable," she pronounced dramatically.

Didi stared at her in confusion. "What was inevitable?"

"The murder."

"Why was it inevitable?"

"Karmic retribution, that's why. Because that field is cursed."

"Oh, come on, Rose!" She shook off the other girl's grip.

"Listen, Didi. Seven years ago, in that same field, a witch was murdered. And now . . . karmic retribution. Don't you see?"

"What is all this about a witch?"

"Her name was Ida Day."

"Where did you get all this stuff from?" Didi asked, scoffing.

"I have my sources."

"Ha! It was Harland Frick, wasn't it? He's the one who fed you this silly story."

"Maybe."

Didi sighed. Harland Frick, a onetime dairy farmer who now owned the town health food store, collected local history, myth, and gossip as a hobby. Much of what he collected was sheer fantasy.

"Listen to me, Rose. Ida Day was no witch. She was an old woman who scratched out a living renting beehives to apple farmers and making up home remedies for people with a sore throat. She was definitely not a witch."

"Did you know her personally?" Rose said defiantly.

"Not really," Didi admitted.

"So! She could well have dabbled in witchcraft without your knowing it."

"She was no witch, Rose," Didi said wearily.

"That field was haunted by her mysterious murder, Didi. I'm telling you. Satan always strikes twice."

"You're beginning to sound like a lunatic, Rose. The murder wasn't at all mysterious. And what does Satan have to do with anything? I remember the killing very well. I was still in school in Philadelphia. My mother wrote me a long letter about what happened.

"One night Ida came home and surprised a young man ransacking her place. She ran into the neighboring field—Lubin's Field—for safety. But the thief followed her there, caught up with her, and killed her.

"They caught him right away. And he confessed, for Pete's sake. He was living down the road in a drug treatment facility. He said he didn't mean to kill the old lady. He just panicked. They sent him to prison for a long time. End of story."

"Are you sure that's what happened, Doc?"

"Am I sure? Well, yeah . . . I mean, no. I mean, of course I wasn't there, Rose. I didn't actually see it with my own eyes. But I believe what my mother wrote to me."

Rose, in a patronizing gesture, patted her gently on the arm. "You know, Didi, there are at least five ways to peel an apple," she said in a grandmotherly fashion. Then she padded off to brew the herbal tea, in which Didi had no interest at all.

The sight that greeted Charlie Gravis when the old saddler Rexall dropped him at the foot of the gravel path leading to Badian's barn was so beautiful that Charlie could only stand there, drinking it in.

Badian's herd was in the pasture. The sun had come out very strong. A wind was swirling the scent of sweet spring grass all around.

Best of all, there was Isaac Badian himself, leaning on a fence, staring at his cows, his face lined and grim as ever. Isaac never smiled. But he never cried either.

It's a beautiful scene, Charlie thought wistfully. This is the way I wanted to die—outdoors, in my pasture, watching my herd. But that dream was gone.

Charlie walked toward his old friend, whom he hadn't even seen in more than a year, much less conversed with. Isaac saw him coming. He squinted at old Charlie and he took a small, blunt cigar out of his shirt pocket, unwrapped it, and lit up.

"Just passing by?" he asked.

"Dropped out of a balloon," Charlie said, "and landed right here on this poor imitation of a dairy farm."

"So you're one of those aliens they talk about.

Didn't know they traveled by balloon nowa-
days."

"You got the picture, Ike."

"The only balloon you ever saw was in the
mirror after you had been hit with a rye
whiskey bottle, Charles Gravis."

"That is unfriendly."

Badian took out a fresh cigar and handed it to
Charlie. They stood together silently for a long
while, shoulder to shoulder, smoking their cig-
ars, staring out at the animals, several of whom
stared back.

"Spring is a bitch," Badian finally said, to no
one in particular.

"I was at the poker game. Rexall told me you
got some trouble."

"Yep. I got some trouble."

"He said 'contamination.' I said, 'What the
hell kind of contamination?' He said, 'How the
hell should I know?' "

Badian snuffed out his cigar and replaced it
in his pocket. Charlie followed suit.

Badian walked to the barn, Charlie right behind him.

The dairy farmer swung open the wide
doors. "Take a look," he said. Charlie stepped
inside ahead of Badian.

Everything *seemed* as it ought to be. The stalls,
the runners, the milkers; everything seemed in
perfect order.

"So?" Charlie asked.

"You hear anything funny?" Ike asked.

Charlie listened. He went on listening for some time. No, he couldn't hear a thing that was funny. He looked at Ike and shrugged.

"Close your eyes and listen," Badian said. "Old people can't hear with their eyes open."

Charlie closed his eyes and listened. Yes! Now he did hear something distinctive. A humming. Or a chirping. Or both.

He opened his eyes. "What is it, Ike?"

Badian pointed to a ledge just behind Charlie.

"Oh my God! Lay me down again!"

It was all Charlie could say when he looked at the ledge and saw about thirty field mice happily chattering away as if they were having a tea party.

"Every see anything like that, Charlie?"

"Not in a long time, no."

"It's a plague. Thousands of field mice and voles and moles and ground squirrels. They're all over. In the feed. In the machinery. In the stalls. Milk yield is down a third. A third! The barn cat has disappeared. I can't put poison down in here. Traps don't even make a dent."

"After a warm, wet winter, sometimes it happens," Charlie said.

"I know why it happens, Charlie. But I don't know what to do about it. I hear it's even worse in Greene and Delaware counties."

Charlie stared at the council of field mice. They seemed to be planning something. Strange little creatures with their tufted ears like antennae.

"I need a pied piper," Ike said.

"They're expensive," Charlie noted.

"I'll pay what it takes. The problem is there ain't no such thing as a pied piper."

Charlie agreed. But something carnal in him stirred.

Chapter 3

An angry Mrs. Tunney stood in the doorway of Trent Tucker's small room in the so-called servants' wing of the sprawling Nightingale house. She had interrupted one of his evening fantasies—about beautiful women and beautiful rifles.

"Why didn't you take the trash to the dump this afternoon?" she demanded.

Trent Tucker sat up, a bit confused. "I forgot," he finally said, more a question than an answer.

"You'd forget your head if it wasn't screwed on. You're lucky Miss Quinn didn't see it."

He swung his feet onto the floor. Mrs. Tunney always cowed him.

She poked her head out of the room and called down the hall: "Abigail! You're going to the dump with Trent Tucker."

Then she poked her head back in and said, "I'm sending Abby with you so you don't end up in that stupid bar drinking beer all night with your friends."

Tucker grinned. "I don't have enough money on me to buy a Pepsi."

"Lord! Are you complaining again? Miss Quinn feeds you and puts clothes on your back and keeps a roof over your head. And now you're bellyaching that you don't have enough money. For what you do around here, young man, if I was Miss Quinn I'd make you sleep in the barn with my horse. And feed you the same way."

She stormed out and into the kitchen.

Trent Tucker hurried outside and began loading the full trash bags on the pickup. It was almost dark and starting to drizzle. The yard dogs yapped playfully at his heels as he worked. When he finished the loading, Abigail was already in the passenger seat. They drove off.

Didi, upstairs, seated in her mother's rocker in her mother's old bedroom, heard the truck pull away.

She assumed it was Trent Tucker going off to meet his friends for some carousing. She didn't give it a second thought because she was deep in a most enjoyable book.

She had originally planned to catch up on her professional reading that evening. A stack of veterinary journals sat waiting on the floor by the rocker. But the mail had brought a book from a used bookstore in New York City, one she had ordered months ago: *The Elephant and the Kangaroo*, by T.H. White.

Didi had as a child read all of White's King Arthur fantasies. When she grew up she read with the same joy his books on falconry and hawking. And she had always wanted to get her hands on *Elephant*, which was long out of print.

Once she started reading, she was hooked. She rocked and laughed and groaned. The book is the first-person narrative of a poor English writer living with an even poorer Irish farming couple deep in bog country. Everyone in the story is somewhere between eccentricity and psychosis—including the writer's dog—an Irish setter who steals baby chicks and rabbits and takes them into the writer's bed each night. It seems that the dog is lonely and likes to hear the babies chirping.

To make matters worse, the Archangel Michael climbs down the chimney and demands they build an ark because a new flood is about to occur and the creatures must be saved.

Didi was so entranced by the lunatic goings-on in the book that she had finished a week's ration of chocolate-covered cherries by the time she reached page fifty.

The pickup truck reached the Hillsbrook dump without incident. Abigail stayed inside the vehicle while Trent Tucker pulled the large plastic bags off the truck and flung them down into the ravine.

Then he climbed back into the pickup and headed for home.

Just as they were driving past Lubin's Field, where the Blessing of the Beasts had almost taken place, Abigail told him in a low voice, "Stop."

Trent ignored her. He wasn't being mean. It was just that no one ever listened to Abigail. Everyone knew she was two bales short of a full hayloft. She often made little comments that indicated she was on a different planet. In short, she was a strange girl. In addition, she had a habit of getting herself involved with some very bizarre men friends—often dangerous ones. On a trip with Miss Quinn to a monastery that bred pedigree dogs, she had seduced a monk and then been arrested for his murder. Although she had eventually been cleared, it just reinforced the local belief that one had to be kind to little Abigail with the lovely voice—but not to pay much attention to her flights of fancy.

So Trent Tucker ignored her soft-spoken request. But when she repeated it—"Please stop . . . Please"—he did so.

"What is it, Abigail?"

"Do you hear it?" she asked.

"I don't hear a thing except you," he replied.

"Listen carefully," she insisted.

Trent Tucker couldn't be sure, but he thought there just might have been a noise off in the distance. "What is it?"

"Look!" she called out, pointing across the road.

Trent Tucker stared into the moon-streaked darkness. He could see the wooden structure that had been built for the ministers and dignitaries on Lubin's Field. His eyes focused at last. Now he could see that someone was on the structure—singing or bellowing.

"Who the hell is that?" he asked. Then he gunned the engine, crossed the road, and drove onto the field.

They left the truck about twenty feet from the wooden structure and approached hesitantly on foot.

Standing on the makeshift stage was the poet Burt Conyers. He was roaring drunk. As usual, he was wearing his sheepskin vest, along with tattered sneakers, and the crook of his bamboo cane was around his neck.

In his hand was a small paperback book. He was reciting something from it, but his words were too slurred to understand.

When he realized that he had company, he stopped reading and bellowed out: "It's about time you people showed up. Sit right down."

"Maybe you'd like a lift home?" Trent Tucker offered gently.

"I *am* home, you idiot," he shouted.

Conyers seemed to see Abigail for the first time then. "Is that you, my love? Yes . . . it is you. But you're so pale. So thin. You are like a beautiful slender stalk that cannot take the wind."

He fell heavily to his knees. The wooden stage seemed to be splintered. Trent Tucker pulled Abigail out of harm's way. But the wood held.

Burt Conyers, still on his knees, ripped a page from the small book and thrust it toward Abigail. "Take it, my love. Take it."

She took the paper and ran toward the truck. Trent followed. The two drove home in silence.

"It's a poem," said Abigail as they headed toward the house.

"As long as it's not a speeding ticket. . . ." said Trent.

"I'll give it to Miss Quinn," Abigail said, and ran into the house via the front door.

The knock on the bedroom door woke Didi out of a deep sleep. She had fallen off in the rocker with T.H. White's book in her lap.

"Come in."

Abigail walked in. Didi was startled. Her elves almost never came upstairs.

"We drove by Lubin's Field," the young girl

explained in her halting, fey manner. "The poet was there. He was drunk, Miss Quinn. And he was reading to the wind. He gave me this poem. You like poems, don't you, Miss Quinn?"

And with that, a very long speech for Abigail, she pushed the sheet of paper into Didi's hands and ran out, closing the door behind her.

Didi looked down at the paper. It seemed to be the last facing page of an old privately printed chapbook. The other side of the page was blank.

She read the poem, titled "Illusion":

> The pines are crowned with snow from
>   the canyons of paradise;
> The bamboo sings with the wind from a
>   frigid hell;
> At midnight the moon rises high. But
>   who is there to see?
> Come, my love. Tap me on the lips. You
>   will get nectar or death!

Didi read it again. Kind of sad. Kind of strange. She liked it. She stuck the page inside the White book as a bookmark.

Then she read a one-year-old veterinary journal, took a bath, and went to sleep.

At midnight she was again awakened by a knock on the door.

It was Mrs. Tunney this time. "You must come downstairs—quick!" she said excitedly.

Didi, not yet fully awake, grabbed a bathrobe and followed the older woman down the stairs.

The front door was open. Didi stepped out into the darkness. It took her a full ten seconds to realize who it was she was facing.

Rose Vigdor was standing in the yard. Her face was almost luminous with fear. Her entire body was trembling from the weight of a limp Aretha in her arms.

Didi rushed to her friend, then stopped suddenly. The German shepherd's head and shoulders were awash in blood.

Allie Voegler brought the binoculars up to his eyes and adjusted the center wheel to bring the surveillance site into focus. It was a fact, an embarrassing one, that he had borrowed the powerful glasses from the state police barracks. But an eight-man force like the Hillsbrook Police Department couldn't be expected to own state-of-the-art surveillance equipment. Or even know how to conduct surveillance.

The car was parked about 300 yards from the tent that served as Sonny James's domicile. Allie had picked the closest hillock that would allow an unimpeded sight line.

The surveillance had started at nine. It was now thirty minutes past midnight. Forty min-

utes ago one of the three white males had left.
He had not yet returned. Inside now were
Sonny, the other male, Sonny's girlfriend Paula,
and an unidentified white female.

Allie put the glasses down. On a real surveillance he would have brought along long-range
cameras so that he could photograph everyone
in the tent. That would be standard operating
procedure. But Allie wasn't really watching the
tent; he was waiting for Sonny James to make a
move.

The white male who had left forty minutes
ago came back carrying several bottles of beer.
Allie picked up the binoculars, zeroed in on the
man's armload, and read the label on one of
them—Heineken Dark. He lay the glasses aside
again.

Would Sonny "jump"?

The rationale behind the surveillance was
based on that premise—that Sonny would jump
because Allie had frightened him.

But the hip bone was connected to the thigh
bone and the thigh bone to . . . In other words,
whether or not Sonny would flee had to depend
on the validity of a particular *scenario*. It wasn't
too persuasive but it was the only one he had.

Scene One: John Breitland and the Animal
Welfare League close down Orin Rafael's
boarding stable.

Scene Two: Rafael publicly threatens John Breitland.

Scene Three: Rafael hires Sonny James to put a bullet through Breitland's head.

Scene Four: Sonny drives his pickup to Lubin's Field. He realizes he's made an error: the truck still has its easily traceable old-fashioned winter tires. He drives the truck back and forth over the ground to obscure the tire tracks. Then he murders Breitland.

Scene Five: Sonny changes the tires to standard all-weather radials and then hides the snow tires and weapon.

Scene Six: Orin Rafael comes back from New York City, where he's been staying in a hotel to establish his alibi. He pays Sonny the murder fee.

Scene Seven: Sonny is happy and safe. But then he is paid a visit by two Hillsbrook police officers. They ask him about the tires and guns. He lies about both. They want to conduct a search. When he refuses, they leave.

Scene Eight: Now Sonny is frightened. If he hasn't already done so, he now has to destroy all the evidence. Now he has to jump.

Allie had gone over the scenario again and again in his own mind. It made sense. But it was flimsy, very flimsy. Made out of matchsticks. One puff and it came tumbling down.

Allie had investigated a number of murders

over the past eight years. But nothing like this. Murder in Hillsbrook meant booze or lunacy. A dairy farmer about to lose his place wakes up one morning and blows his wife away with a shotgun blast; then botches his own suicide. Or a young kid has one drink too many, gets into an argument at a rest stop, and cracks a skull with a baseball bat.

But John Breitland's murder was an assassination. A cold-blooded, professional hit. An altogether different kettle of fish.

Allie brought the glasses up again. He could see that the unidentified female was now dancing by herself; a kind of slow grind. No one in the large tent seemed to be paying much attention to her.

He moved his glasses to focus on Sonny James, who was drinking beer from the bottle and smoking casually on a decrepit sofa. Allie wondered if James had been in that tent all winter. How do you winterize a structure like that? Probably with cinder blocks.

He brought the glasses down. There was another problem with the scenario: Sonny James himself.

The young man was a wild one. But a paid assassin? Hard to say. Apart from his juvenile rap sheet, Sonny had been arrested and convicted only once. And Allie had been the arresting officer. But the circumstances of the case were peculiar, to say the least.

Three young men from Columbia County had hijacked a huge propane truck. Probably on a lark. But then they decided to try to sell the propane. One of them contacted Sonny James for advice. He told them to put the gas in small tanks and then he, Sonny, would sell them to trailer owners who use propane for heating and cooking.

The three young men blew themselves up while transferring the gas. One died. One required skin grafts. One suffered only minor injuries. Sonny was arrested on conspiracy to sell stolen goods. He got eighteen months probation and a thousand dollar fine.

Sonny James a hired killer? Allie just didn't know about that one. Still, the scenario was logical.

He peered through the binoculars once more. The unidentified woman was still dancing, but her mode of moving had become frankly erotic, almost as if she were doing a strip.

Voegler pulled the glasses savagely from his face. He felt a sudden lash of shame. For a brief moment he had fantasized that the woman doing the suggestive dance routine was Didi Nightingale.

This is no good, he thought. No damn good at all. There seemed to be no end to his frustration . . . his misery . . . where Didi was concerned. He couldn't make love to her and he couldn't move on. He was in a trap. Where was Didi right now? In bed, of course. Why hadn't she called him? And why hadn't he been able to call her?

He recalled grimly what that Philadelphia detective had told him after Allie introduced him to Didi. The guy's name was Pratt, if Allie remembered right.

Pratt said that Didi has a secret life; that Allie really hadn't a clue about her desires. Allie had interpreted that to mean she had a secret lover somewhere and that was the reason she did not reciprocate his affection. But he knew in his heart that that wasn't true. He knew that Didi loved *him*. He knew she did want him.

He picked up the binoculars.

"Jump, Sonny! Jump, you son of a bitch!" he muttered angrily to himself.

"Where am I? What's going on?" Rose had awakened suddenly. She stood straight up and stared around down uncomprehendingly at the sofa she had been sleeping on.

"Take it easy, Rose," Didi said comfortingly. "You're in my clinic. I gave you a sedative."

"But Aretha! Where's Aretha?"

"She's fine," Didi assured her. "Look over there. See?"

The shepherd was lying on the examining table at the far end of the clinic. She was sleeping peacefully, her back legs twitching just a bit. Her neck was heavily bandaged.

"Thank God," Rose said and fell back onto the sofa.

"The bullet went right through the nape of her neck," explained Didi. "There was a lot of blood. But that's all. I cleaned it all off and sewed her up. She'll be fine. I knocked her out with a strong pain killer."

"I thought she was dead, Didi. There was just so much blood."

"Sometimes it's better to be old than young. In this case, age worked in Aretha's favor. Young German shepherds don't have all that loose hanging flesh at the neck."

Didi sat beside Rose, inspecting her own hands. She had scrubbed down after sewing Aretha up, but the scrub soap had left an ugly residue.

"Tell me what happened, Rose."

"I was fast asleep. The dogs woke me, carrying on something awful. When they calmed down a little, I could hear a funny noise outside."

"What kind of noise do you mean?"

"Clicking."

"Be more specific, Rose, please."

"*Click-click. Click-click. Click-click!* Like that."

Didi walked quietly from the sofa to her desk and began to rummage through the top drawer. She pulled out an object and proudly displayed it.

"What is that?" Rose asked.

"Jiminey Cricket!" Didi replied, as though this were explanation enough for anyone. She brought the little metal object over to Rose on the sofa and positioned it near Rose's ear. *Click-click!*

Rose snatched the thing out of Didi's fingers. "Jim who? Didi, what the hell is this?"

"Don't you city girls know anything?" Didi said, laughing. "Jiminey Cricket—from *Pinocchio*, I think. You know . . . Disney. Well, anyway, for years you used to get them in boxes of breakfast cereal. My mother gave this one to me when I was just a little kid."

Rose handed the toy back. "That's what I heard. Sounds crazy, doesn't it?"

"Not really," said Didi. "Tell me what happened next."

"I walked outside, to see where the noise was coming from, and what it could have been that was making the dogs so worked up. I headed toward the road. And then I heard a shot and a yelp at almost the same instant. And my poor Aretha went down. I guess I kind of lost it. I freaked out."

"And you didn't see anyone?"

"No, no one."

Didi worked the clicker a few times. Then she said, "Do you know who uses these things now, Rose? Dog trainers. It seems that nothing gets a dog's attention like that clicking sound. Nobody knows why. But it sure does the trick."

"You mean someone wanted to kill Aretha? Someone was watching us, deliberately trying to lure her out so they could shoot her?"

"It looks that way."

"My God! They've always hated me here, haven't they? I never did fit in. Everybody in Hillsbrook thinks I'm crazy. I knew that. But I never thought they would target a poor helpless dog."

"You're talking nonsense now, Rose. There are only two reasons people in Dutchess County shoot dogs. One: if they run deer. Two: if they kill livestock."

"Aretha wouldn't do either of those things. There's never been even a hint of that kind of behavior."

Didi heard Mrs. Tunney rattling around the kitchen, starting to prepare her eternal and infernal pot of oatmeal. The entire night had slipped away. It was morning.

She punched the little clicker again.

"Please don't do that anymore," Rose begged.

"Oh, sorry." Didi nodded her apology. But a very strange thought was beginning to brew. What if the shooter was after Rose, not Aretha?

Rose was correct in thinking that most of Hillsbrook considered her nature girl aspirations ridiculous. But there was no hatred of her. No, it had to be something else. There had to be some other explanation.

"Rose, have you been talking about your theory lately?"

"What theory?"

"That the tragedy in Lubin's Field happened because Ida Day died there. And that Ida Day was a witch."

"I mentioned it to a few people, I guess. And Harland Frick, who agrees with me, might have been talking to people about it."

Didi was silent.

"But so what?" asked Rose combatively. "So what if I told people about it? It's what I believe!"

"Maybe that's why someone took a shot . . . at you."

"Oh, damn. I knew it! I knew you were going to say that. But what kind of lunatic does something like that? Do you try to kill someone just because she claims a field is haunted?" Rose asked desperately.

"What if your belief that Ida was a witch and the field where she was murdered in haunted is the key to the Breitland assassination, Rose? What if Aretha was hit in error? What if the person who fired that shot is Breitland's murderer?"

"But what does one thing have to do with the other? All I said was that something bad was bound to happen in that field because the place is haunted."

"That's right. That was all you said to *me*."

"It's all I said to anyone!" she protested.

"Are you frightened, Rose?"

"Damn right, I am."

"So am I," Didi said quietly. "Particularly if there is some connection between the two killings."

"But I never said there was. It didn't even occur to me."

"I don't think it occurred to anyone else either. Until now."

"What should I do?" Rose asked.

"Have breakfast. Have some of Mrs. Tunney's oatmeal. I'll check on you later. I've got to go see someone."

"Now?"

"Yes, now." Didi looked over at the large wall clock. Five forty-five a.m. She would skip her yoga exercises this morning. She walked over to the examining table where Aretha lay and checked on her patient. The bitch was fine.

Both victims—Aretha on the table and Rose on the sofa—and in fact the entire household—had gotten a good night's sleep, in spite of all the excitement. Everyone except Didi, that is.

And now she was too confused to even think of sleep. She needed some answers.

On her drive into town to find Allie Voegler, she realized there was an alternative to the idea that Rose had been the true target of the attack: The shooter might have meant only to wound the animal as a warning to Rose to keep her mouth shut. But to keep her mouth shut about what? It had to be connected to Ida Day. That had to be part of the answer.

Didi's anxiety increased as she got closer to the village. Her closest friend and her animals were at risk. Great risk.

Allie Voegler lived on the third and last floor of a dingy building on a dingy side street of the village. The ground floor of the building was occupied by stores.

He answered the bell immediately and was waiting for her, half dressed, on the landing. He was both shocked and pleased by her visit.

"What will the neighbors think?" he asked mischievously.

"That we're lovers," she said flatly.

Allie ushered her into his small kitchen and poured out two cups of coffee from an old drip pot. She sat across the small table from him.

"You getting ready for work?" Didi asked.

"No. I wasn't dressing; I was *un*dressing

when you buzzed. I worked last night. Just got in."

Didi sipped her coffee. He looked weary, she thought, and he had lost weight. She felt the same contradictory feelings she always felt in his presence—attraction and repulsion. A desire to embrace him and to flee from him. It was, and always had been, a dreadful and frustrating dilemma. But, she knew, he felt none of that ambiguity. He wanted her unconditionally. And that fed into her wariness. Sooner or later, she knew, she would have to sleep with him or end the relationship altogether.

He reached his large, powerful hand across the table. She studied the hand minutely. Allie was a powerful man. That, above all, was what made her wary of him: he was this huge, imposing being with an almost desperate need for her. Like one of the big, helpless animals she treated. She was the only thing that stood between the wounded creatures and death.

"Why are you here, Didi?" he asked frankly. "You seem to be avoiding me lately."

"I'm here for help."

He looked disappointed.

"It's my friend Rose Vigdor," Didi said. "She's in trouble, I think."

Allie laughed softly. "Is anything else new?"

"I mean it, Allie. I think her life may be in danger."

"Are you for real? In danger from who?"

"Well, somebody shot one of her dogs last night."

"Killed?"

"No. She's okay. I patched her up."

"You report it?"

"No."

"Why not?"

"Because there's something strange about it. Really strange. The dog might not have been the real target. The shooting might have been a warning."

"To who?"

"To Rose, of course."

"But a warning against what?"

"That's the weird part. Rose has learned some crazy things—or thinks she has learned them. Anyway, she's been going around saying that Ida Day, the old woman who was killed in Lubin's Field all those years ago, was some kind of witch."

"What? That's crazy!" he scoffed.

"Yes, yes, I know. But you know Rose. You know how she gets about things. Anyway, it looks like maybe someone thinks she's made a connection between the two murders."

He pulled his hand away then. "What two murders?"

"Ida Day and John Breitland. They were murdered in the same field, remember?"

Allie raised himself halfway out of his chair. Then he reached across the table with that same strong hand, plucked her coffee cup from her grasp, and flung it toward the far wall. Connecting with the porcelain sink, the cup shattered.

The violence was so sudden and explosive that Didi leapt out of her seat and backed away from the table. "What is the matter with you, Allie Voegler?" she shouted. "Have you lost your—"

"You listen to me, Madam Veterinarian! You just stick to your milk cows and stop talking about things you know nothing about. There is no connection between those two murders. None. That old lady was murdered a long time ago in a botched robbery by a junkie kid from Sun House. We found Ida's stuff in the kid's room. He confessed! Breitland was killed in a carefully planned assassination. And we think we know who planned it. And who carried it out. No connection. *Nada.* Nothing. You hear me?"

He had punctuated his outburst with his fist, beating it on the table.

"Maybe we can talk when you calm down, Allie," she said and walked swiftly out of the apartment. He did not say a word as she left.

Once on the street, she just stood near the jeep. She was trembling from Allie's furious outburst. What could she have said to trigger such a reaction?

Didi started to breathe in and out like she did each morning during her yoga exercises. Calm would return shortly, she knew.

As she stood there in the morning sun, she wondered why the name of a long-dead old woman kept surfacing—and with such tumultuous results. Ida Day. Ida Day. Ida Day.

Then she climbed into the jeep and drove to the drug rehabilitation center known as Sun House. The director was Jed Benteen. Didi had treated his chocolate Lab, Jock, several times. Benteen liked her. And as for Didi the feeling was mutual.

A stroke of luck. A stroke of luck. That's all Charlie Gravis could think of when he awoke and realized that there would be no rounds that morning. He listened sympathetically as Mrs. Tunney told him about the dog in the clinic and how an exhausted Miss Quinn had just driven off without a word. Yes, he was very sympathetic while consuming his oatmeal.

But the moment he left the kitchen he grabbed Trent Tucker by the arm and promised the tortures of hell if the young man didn't drive him immediately to Blanche Hopper's place twenty miles distant.

Trent Tucker complied. But the trip took

much longer than contemplated because Charlie couldn't remember just where Blanche Hopper's house was within the confines of the incorporated village of Chester, south and west of Hillsbrook.

When he finally did find it, he realized the confusion stemmed from the indisputable fact that Blanche's little house was now red. When he had last visited it was blue.

He ordered Trent Tucker to wait for him in the pickup.

"Is this a robbery? Should I keep the motor running?" the younger man asked.

Tucker's joke was not appreciated.

Charlie knocked boldly on the front door. A woman on the porch of the neighboring house stared at him suspiciously. The houses in these parts were ridiculously small, Charlie thought.

"Oh my!"

Someone had at last answered the door.

"What a delightful surprise, Charlie!" Blanche Hopper embraced him tightly for a long moment and then pulled him inside. She and Charlie were either second or third cousins. Neither was sure. Blanche was one of those women whose hair kept getting whiter as she aged . . . whose back kept bending . . . but whose language got younger, more melodious, more unpredictable.

She sat Charlie down in the guest chair and

brought him a glass of cold water and some fruit. "Coffee is being prepared," she announced. Then she tapped him on the knee and asked, "Well, cousin, what have you been up to?"

Charlie drank the water down, then began to lay out the current adventures of the entire Nightingale household. Blanche listened in a kind of rapture.

Then he interrupted his own monologue: "Where's Yam?" he asked. "I don't see Yam. Has anything happened to him?"

She shook her head vigorously. "Oh no! He's fine. Since he's gotten his own room, he doesn't care much for visitors."

"His own room?"

"Yes. I fixed up that storehouse behind the kitchen for him."

Blanche walked halfway to the kitchen.

"Coffee will be ready soon," she said.

Then she called out: "Yammy, you have a visitor."

She sat down across from Charlie, folded her arms, and waited. Charlie did not resume his Nightingale house monologue. The world was waiting for Yam.

Then in walked Yam, to investigate the turmoil.

He was an aged, mustard-colored cat with

very small ears, very yellow eyes, and very large toe pads.

He stretched, then walked over to Charlie and checked him out.

"Doesn't he look fine?" Blanche gushed. "It's hard to believe, Charlie, that it was almost three years ago that you gave Yam to me. He is just the sweetest pussycat in the world."

Gravis narrowed his eyes considerably and stared at Yam, who was staring right back.

"Yes, time flies," he said. The cat had belonged to one of Charlie's friends—Al Hobson. When Al died Charlie was charged with getting rid of all the animals and objects so the property could be sold.

"We love each other to pieces, Yam and me," Blanche said happily. Then she cried out: "My God! The coffee!" And hurried into the kitchen.

Charlie made sure Blanche was otherwise engaged and not looking toward the living room. Then he bent over and whispered to the cat.

"You are a helluva actor. She doesn't have the slightest clue who you are."

Yam twitched his little black nose and cocked his ears. He started to walk away a bit stiff-legged.

Blanche returned. "Just a minute more for the coffee, Charlie," she announced. She picked Yam up and sat down with him on her lap. She scratched his neck softly while she spoke. "Isn't he a darling?"

"He looks pretty healthy," Charlie noted.

"Hasn't been sick a day."

"And his coat looks real good," Blanche added. "I brush him three times a week. He loves to be brushed. You know, Charlie, some of my friends say his coat is an ugly color. I mean, it's almost yellow. He does look like a yam. But I think it's pretty. You just have to get used to it."

"It's pretty, all right," Charlie agreed.

"And he'll eat anything, you know," she said proudly.

"No kidding?"

"He's the least finicky cat I've ever seen in my life. He eats wet food and dry food. Just any kind. He'll eat chicken, fish, beef, turkey. He'll try anything once—even turnips mashed with butter."

"You don't say?"

Charlie sat back in his chair. Old Al Hobson would be laughing in his grave if he could see this sight.

Blanche Hopper hadn't the slightest idea that the dear little pussycat she was cradling in her lap was none other than Wyatt Earp. Yep, that was his real name. The name Al Hobson had given him.

And he was called that because he was the greatest mouser in Dutchess County. A lean, mean mouse-killing machine. The champion rodent hater in the county, and maybe the whole damn state.

Blanche let Yam down, went into the kitchen, and came back with a tray groaning with hot coffee, cups, spoons, light cream, brown lump sugar, and sliced pound cake on a plate. She prepared Charlie's mug, following his instructions on how much of this and how much of that to add. Yam looked on for a moment, then headed back to his room.

"Delicious coffee," Charlie claimed after his first sip. He was lying. It had that metallic "decaf" taste.

"It's so good to see you, Charlie," she said. "You have to visit more often."

"Oh, I will, Cousin Blanche. From now on." He drank more coffee and reached for a piece of cake. "I promise."

Blanche soon began one of her long, complicated stories about her frustrating encounters with the medical profession.

Charlie seemed to be listening intently, but he wasn't. No, his thoughts were elsewhere. His efforts to conduct a lucrative, clandestine herbal medicine business out of the Nightingale barn had been undone through betrayal. His attempt to win the New York State lottery had failed because he had selected the wrong partner. But this new plan of his—this was foolproof.

Charlie Gravis was about to become the Pied Piper of Dutchess County.

For a hefty fee he would make any dairy operation field mouse free.

He put the coffee mug down and folded his hands on his chest, deep in thought. One problem remained: how to borrow Wyatt Earp?

In the late 1970s and early 1980s many drug and alcohol rehab centers began to do business in the Hillsbrook area. Old mansions were purchased and refitted as clinics. And they quickly filled with, for the most part, well-heeled addicts of one kind or another.

The clinic boom tapered off in the late '80s, much to the relief of the townspeople. Several facilities closed down. One had become a county museum.

Sun House, however, was one of the few that survived and indeed continued to thrive with a mix of alcoholics and drug addicts whose treatment was paid for by health insurance plans. The "alkies" usually remained in the programs for six weeks, while twelve weeks was the average stay for the "druggies." The staff at Sun House was top notch. Treatment was heavily nutritional after the traditional withdrawal phase, during which the patients were sedated.

A security guard at the gate waved Didi through. The main driveway was framed on either side by beautiful slender pin oaks just about to start their spring bursts. Didi parked her jeep in the Staff Only section and walked right into the director's office without knocking.

Jed Benteen was at his desk, writing. He didn't even look up, just waved to signal that he would be with his visitor in a moment.

Jock, the friendly Labrador, came out to greet her. Didi grabbed his muzzle and played with him roughly.

"Dr. Nightingale! I didn't know it was you," Benteen said, a little flustered, as he pushed his chair away from the desk. He was on the short side, well built, with sandy hair, and about fifty years old. He wore thick tortoiseshell glasses.

Didi wasted no time with preliminaries. "Mr. Benteen, I want you to tell me about that patient at Sun House who murdered Ida Day."

Benteen's face registered his surprise. Then he looked at her as if to evaluate her behavior. Was she using some sort of substance?

"You do know what I'm talking about, don't you?" she asked.

Benteen recovered. "Of course. The young man's name was Lou Mosely."

"Was?"

He died in a jailhouse fight two years ago."

"Oh. I didn't know that."

Both Didi and Benteen fell into momentary silence.

"Can you," she resumed, "tell me something about him? About the murder, I mean."

"Why don't you ask Allie Voegler? Isn't he a friend of yours? He's the one who made the case against the boy."

"I tried to. He didn't want to talk about it."

"That isn't a tremendous surprise." Benteen laughed wickedly. "If I were him I wouldn't want to talk about it either."

"What do you mean by that?"

"The boy was innocent," he said simply.

"But I thought he confessed."

"That's right. He confessed. He confessed to the murder. He said that he was burglarizing the old lady's cottage. She came in, she saw him, she ran into the neighboring field screaming. He tried to shut her up, panicked, hit her with a rock or a pipe. Then he hid the stolen goods in his room here at Sun House."

"Well?" Didi said. "That's pretty clear."

Benteen moved back closer to his desk, picked up a pencil and spun it on the desktop.

"Sure is clear," he said. "Why shouldn't it be? Your friend Voegler, with the help of the local D.A., scripted that confession. Lou Mosely signed it because they said if he didn't sign they'd press for Murder One—and get it. Life without parole. This way, with his confession, he'd only have to serve ten years. It didn't matter that he was innocent, they told him. The evidence would prove him guilty. He had to make the best of a bad situation. The kid was too frightened and too weak to tough it out. Then he went and got himself killed in prison. Yes, Dr. Nightingale, if I were your friend Allie Voegler I would be reluctant to discuss that case. And I'd also have trouble sleeping all these years. Particularly since it was the Ida Day murder that made Voegler a detective—the first plainclothes detective in the history of the Hillsbrook Police Department."

Didi listened, stunned. She didn't know what or whom to believe or disbelieve. This Benteen was right about Allie being disturbed by the case. That much was obvious. He had never said a word about the Day case to her. Yet he had spoken about dozens of others. And he had never reacted so violently as he had this morning when she brought up the notion that there might be a connection between the two killings in Lubin's Field.

But she had no idea as to whether Allie had borne this cross legitimately, or illegitimately. Why believe in Mosely's innocence just because Benteen announced it?

"Tell me, Mr. Benteen, if you believed so strongly in Lou Mosely's innocence at the time

. . . and the boy was so alone and frightened
. . . why didn't you help him out?"

Benteen laughed bitterly. "Were you in Hillsbrook at the time, Dr. Nightingale?"

"No. I was away at school."

"I thought as much. Otherwise, you'd know
what was going on here. After the murder and
the arrest everybody wanted to close the clinics—all of them. To kick them out of the town
because our patients were really drug-crazed
killers. I am afraid I acted like any other cow-
ard. I distanced myself from the boy to save my
livelihood. And believe me, I deserve to burn in
hell for it."

Didi thanked him for his honesty and left
quickly, without even saying good-bye to Jock.
She just wanted to get out of there and talk to
Allie.

There was a pay phone right outside the
clinic gate. She dialed his home number. There
was no answer. Maybe, she thought, he was too
upset to sleep and had gone into work. She
called the station house, but he wasn't there either.

She drove to the tavern on Route 44. It was
just opening for the day.

Allie Voegler was the only customer at the
bar, beer in hand.

Didi sat down two stools away from him. He
looked over at her but said nothing.

"I was just passing by," she said.

He shrugged. It was, she realized, his pathetic attempt at an apology for his behavior earlier.

But she didn't want or need an apology. She wanted to help him. There was so much confusion and misery in his eyes.

She couldn't bear to watch him because it was her questions that had put those things in his eyes, her probing that had reopened what must have been a very painful old wound. If Benteen was right, Allie had sent an innocent boy to prison . . . to his death . . . and he had profited by that terrible act.

Didi turned on the bar stool and looked out of the window. Life turned on a dime. Everything had been going well. And now, suddenly, her two best friends in Hillsbrook—Allie and Rose—were in deep trouble.

She got off the seat and walked over to him, burying her face in his shoulder. Allie stiffened. She stepped back and ran her hand through his hair. She wanted to tell him that she was going to get her friends out of this mess . . . both messes . . . but she couldn't get the words out.

Allie took a long drink of beer. He pulled her close and whispered in her ear: "See what happens when you try to bless animals in Lubin's Field?"

Didi walked out.

Chapter 4

Charlie walked into the barn just as the milking was finished. His practical eye made a quick count—sixteen cows in the north stalls, nine in the south stalls. Twenty-five dairy cows in all, out of a total of forty-eight stall spaces.

Ike Badian was scrubbing down the aluminum milking machines. His assistant, a kid named Gary, was moving the raw milk toward the loading dock to await the milk truck.

The situation was not good, Charlie knew. Usually, after milking, cows were placid. They snacked, they snoozed, they ruminated, they sighed.

These animals, however, were on edge. They kept shifting around and bellowing and giving each other nervous stares.

It was obvious to Charlie what was disturbing the cows. The barn was awash with tiny little rustlings. Most of the field mice couldn't really be seen. They had insinuated themselves beneath and between everything.

Charlie stood there a full five minutes marveling at the infestation before Isaac Badian noticed him.

"You looking for work?" Ike asked jokingly.

"I got work."

"Yeah. But what does that voodoo lady pay you?"

Ike Badian considered all veterinarians to be practitioners of black magic.

"Enough," Charlie answered the question.

The two men walked out of the barn. Badian lit the stub of a cigar.

"I have a proposition for you, Ike."

The dairy farmer squinted his eyes. "The last time someone told me that, Charlie, I had to get married."

"Do you want to hear the proposition or not?"

"Sure. Go ahead."

"For a thousand dollars cash I'll get rid of your problem for you."

"Which problem?"

"The mice. The field mice in the barn. Just the barn, Ike, not the fields."

"How the hell you going to do that, Charlie?"

"I'll do it."

"I don't want no poison laid down in my barn."

"No poison. I promise."

"And traps won't do it."

"Agreed."

"And I *don't* want that voodoo girl snooping around here with her magic potions."

To Ike, all pharmaceutical agents, no matter their level of scientific efficacy, were magic potions.

"No Dr. Nightingale."

"Then how, Charlie?"

"You leave that to me. I figure it'll take about a week."

Badian squinted out across the field and chewed his cigar ferociously.

"A thousand dollars is a lot of money, Charlie."

"Sure it is. Particularly a thousand dollars cash on the barrelhead."

"Too much, Charlie. Maybe six or seven."

"Well," Charlie said, "it was a pleasure doing business—almost doing business—with you, Ike." He started to walk toward Trent Tucker's pickup, still parked by the road. Trent was leaning against a fender, smoking leisurely.

"Wait, Charlie!" Ike called desperately. "Just a minute. Okay. A thousand. But you don't get a dime until the job is finished."

"Fair enough."

The two old men shook hands.

Charlie headed for the truck. He felt absolutely elated. He hadn't seen a thousand dollars cash in a long time. And this would only be the beginning. Soon he'd have his own brand-new van, and painted on it would be HIRE THE PIED PIPER OF HILLSBROOK.

But wait. Just Hillsbrook would be too restrictive. Better make it THE PIED PIPER OF DUTCHESS COUNTY. Yeah, that was better. You can't keep a good man down.

Charlie slowed a bit as he approached the truck. His elation had been dampened, but not much.

He had lied to Badian. Dr. Nightingale *would* be somewhat involved. But only tangentially. She'd never know it, and what she didn't know wouldn't hurt her. So what if he used her name and her prestige to get hold of Wyatt Earp for a few nights? Nobody would be getting hurt. Except, of course, the mice. But they were the ones who started it. They had declared war first.

Didi sat for a long time in her red jeep staring morosely at the simple sign tacked up on the post:

BOARDING STABLE, REASONABLE RATES!

The sign was now irrelevant. Orin Rafael's boarding stables were closed, by law. Why on earth hadn't he taken the sign down?

Her hands were still on the wheel. This was a bizarre situation for her—to be taking matters into her own hands. She usually tried to act by the dictates of reason. And reason usually dictated going slowly . . . acting in concert with others . . . avoiding precipitate actions.

She felt a little frightened, a little excited, and more than a little worried that she might be getting in over her head.

She was also experiencing the weirdest delusion—that she was about to cull a herd.

It was odd that she should have this delusion. She puzzled over it. The thought obviously sprang from an old memory. In the last year of vet school she had gone to a lecture by a vet who had just returned from Africa. He had worked in one of the great Kenyan game preserves. He talked about a culling operation. One elephant herd had grown too large for the food supply and begun to raid farms outside the preserve and eat the crops. It was decided to reduce the size of the herd. His job was to accompany the hunter and point out the lame and the sick, who were to be culled first.

Didi squirmed in her seat. Why did she think she was on a culling operation? Who was she culling? The innocent or the guilty? There was no similarity whatsoever. Someone or something was stalking her friends. And if she didn't find out who and why, her friends would be destroyed. It was very simple. The problem was that whatever or whoever was stalking them was quite invisible and walking an equally invisible tightrope that stretched over seven years between the two murders in Lubin's Field.

She stared at the sign again. Everything has to start right here, she thought. That murderous tightrope ends in Breitland's shattered skull. And the prime suspect is Orin Rafael.

She climbed resolutely out of the jeep, slammed the door shut, and strode toward the now closed stable.

A harsh and angry-sounding voice stopped her in her tracks. "What the hell are you doing here?"

Orin Rafael seemed to have materialized out of nowhere. She hadn't seen him approach. He was carrying a saddle blanket.

"Hello," Didi said, striving to keep her voice light and friendly. She knew Rafael by sight only. She had never done any veterinary work for him. Maybe that nasty tone of voice was the norm for him, just his natural way of speaking. Maybe he was just a salty, short-tempered horseman. Didi had met hundreds of those.

Rafael, thin and rather bloodless looking, was fastidiously dressed and wore a beautiful pair of brown stable boots. An old eye injury made him periodically shield one eye from the strong sunlight. "Did Detective Voegler send you here?" he asked, one hand held close to his face.

"No one sent me, Mr. Rafael," Didi said, her voice still light and sweet. "My name is—"

Rafael suddenly spat, startling her into silence. He looked past Didi's shoulder, as if expecting to see Allie Voegler walking their way.

"I thought maybe," he said ruefully, "Voegler was sending his pet over here to sell me some tickets to the policeman's ball."

"I'd rather be Voegler's pet than Breitland's butcher," she snapped back.

He took a menacing step toward her. For a moment she thought he was going to strike out, but she stood her ground and he reined in his anger.

"Listen to me, girl, whatever your name is. Your friend Voegler identified me as a suspect to the world. He degraded me. He lied about me. Yes, I threatened Breitland, I don't deny it. Because he and his loonies closed me down. But I didn't kill him. I'll tell you something else while I'm about it. Those horses didn't die in my stables because of my negligence. Do you want to know what happened?"

She didn't respond at all. He took her silence as an invitation to continue.

"I got a call from a trainer at a trotting track in Buffalo. He wanted to lay up three of his horses for a month. Wanted the minimum rate—just stall space. A groom was coming down with the horses and he was going to do the feeding and mucking out. The horses and the groom got here. It turned out the groom was a drunk. He doused the feed, by mistake, with some kind of cleaning agent, and the horses died overnight. That is what happened. Do you understand?"

"I'm not interested in why the court closed you down," Didi said.

"Oh no? Why the hell are you here then? You really want to question me about the Breitland murder. Is that it? Listen, I didn't kill John. I knew that man a long long time. When the Hillsbrook Hunt was riding he even used to board some of his horses with me. I had no quarrel with him until I found out he wanted to put me out of business. He took away my livelihood. Don't you people get it? Of course I was mad about it. What do you expect?"

Rather than answer the question, Didi posed one of her own? "Did you know Ida Day?"

"Who?"

"Ida Day."

"Never heard of her. Oh, wait . . . Day . . . Day. You're not talking about the woman who was killed by that dog of a drug addict, are you?"

"Yes."

"Didn't know her. Just remember the name."

"What about Lou Mosely? Did you know him?"

"No. Who is he?"

"That dog of a drug addict, as you called him."

"Of course I didn't know him. What do you think . . ."

Rafael seemed to lose his train of thought, and his terrible anger, just for a moment. He was staring intently at Didi.

"You know," he said slowly, "you bear a very strong resemblance to a young lady who used to ride with the hunt."

"Really?" Didi asked, not much interested in his reminiscences. "Who was she?"

"I don't remember her name."

Didi noticed the little smirk at the corner of the man's mouth. What was this strange man trying to tell her? That she resembled some old lover of his? A lady who used to ride the hounds. It was odd how people in Hillsbrook still seemed fixated on the Hillsbrook Hunt a decade after its demise. She thought of Lilly Donniger and her horse Glowworm, who had been purchased from the Hunt Stables, or so Mrs. Donniger claimed.

"How about Rose Vigdor, Mr. Rafael? You know her?"

He burst into mocking laughter. "Nature Girl, you mean. Now that's really one for the books."

His derision infuriated Didi. She gave him a sharp glance. He went right on with his evil chuckling. Didi tried to visualize him taking aim at the defenseless Aretha, firing a bullet into the poor shepherd's neck. If he had murdered John Breitland, he certainly was capable of hurting an animal.

Rafael didn't stop at ridiculing Rose. He made a lewd joke about her and her menagerie of animals in the ramshackle barn that she called home.

At that moment, Didi knew that she loathed this man. And she wanted to hurt him.

"So, Mr. Rafael," she began, her voice even and pleasant, "you say that John Breitland thought enough of you as a horseman to board some of the hunt horses at your place."

"Yeah. That's right."

"So why did you end up having to take in broken-down trotters all the way from Buffalo?"

"What the hell are you talking about?" he boomed. "The Hillsbrook Hunt closed down nine or ten years ago."

"I know that. But the people who kept their hunting horses at Breitland's obviously needed a place to board those animals after the hunt disbanded. There must be a reason they wouldn't give you the business; they took their horses elsewhere—to places they trusted."

Rafael was fuming. "You don't know what you're talking about! During the last years of the Hillsbrook Hunt most of the members were not

from around here. They were rich people from
Long Island and Connecticut or Pennsylvania.
Who had all the time and money in the world to
play eighteenth-century games. When the hunt
closed down here, they just shipped their horses
to another place, where the hunting action was
still going on."

Didi gave him her own version of his smirk,
which said that he was simply making excuses
for himself, that he couldn't face the fact that
the courts had been justified in closing him
down for incompetence, and that everyone
knew it.

Then she imitated his cruel laughter.

Before he could vent any more of his anger,
Didi turned away from him and sauntered back
to the jeep, not even bothering to say good-bye.

She turned the key in the ignition. Rafael was
still standing where she left him, glowering at
her. She looked at her watch. There was time to
make one house call. She wanted to see how
Glowworm was doing.

"Is it true about Aretha?" Harland Frick asked
the moment Rose entered the health food store.

She nodded affirmatively and sat down on a
huge carton filled with organic peanut butter in
glass jars.

"But she's alive and well and with Didi," she
said.

Just being in the store soothed Rose Vigdor. It was her favorite place in town and Harland Frick her favorite Hillsbrookian besides Didi. He knew more about the area and its people than anyone else—and knew the secret things.

Of course, many people in the town thought this little old man with the broken blood vessels on his nose and the tufts of white hair dotting his almost bald skull was quite mad.

Rose knew better. He was saner than all of them put together.

"Why would anyone shoot Aretha?" Harland asked, sharpening a pencil with a tiny handheld sharpener and then blowing the shavings away from the point.

"Didi says it's because I've been babbling to people about Lubin's Field being haunted."

"So what?"

"Well, she says by doing that I inadvertently made a connection between the two murders that happened in the field. And someone else made that connection. It might even have been the killer himself."

"That friend of yours has a honey of an imagination. What do you think, Rose?"

"I don't know. I'm just scared. Very scared, Harland. What if they come after my dogs again—or me?"

He nodded sympathetically. Then he opened a box that contained small vials of natural skin

cream, made of cucumbers and wildflowers—
and checked them against a bill of lading. He
used the newly sharpened pencil flamboyantly,
as if it were a rapier.

Rose sat quietly, watching the movement of
the pencil with fascination. There was safety in
this place. She shifted her eyes to one of the
aisles where the bags of chips hung.

Was she not Harland Frick's biggest chips
customer? She lived on corn chips, avocado
chips, potato chips, and about twenty other va-
rieties. It seemed now that if it grew in the
ground, it could be made into a chip. She was
waiting patiently for tomato chips. And soon
after that would come cantaloupe.

Her reverie was shattered suddenly by a loud
crash of the door.

And then a shout: "Hello, apothecary!"

It was only the eccentric poet Burt Conyers,
in full regalia, including his bamboo cane.

"I'm not an apothecary, stupid." Harland retorted.

"Has it come to this? The poet laureate of
Dutchess County being called stupid by an old
lush who spent forty years milking cows and to
this day doesn't know what a cow really is."

"If you're the poet laureate of Dutchess
County, I'm Elizabeth Taylor."

"There is a resemblance."

Rose was appalled by the repartee until she
realized there was an undercurrent of affection

between the men. It was just an insult game. That's all.

"Actually," the poet said, "I didn't come in to see you, old man. I was in the bank checking on my investments. . . ."

The poet paused. Then both men burst out laughing. It was obvious that among other things Conyers lived so far below the poverty line that a bank was one place he never walked into.

The poet continued. "And I saw this lovely young woman entering the store. I was afraid for her, being that you're a lecherous old goat, and I wanted to defend her virtue."

He turned to Rose. "And to you I wanted to say how ashamed I am about what happened to your dog. I want to assure you that when we find the monster we will tie him to four horses and pull the bastard apart. Of all the horrors on earth there is none worse than wounding the canine companion of a good woman."

Rose didn't know how to respond. The poet made an attempt at a gallant bow and then stamped out.

Harland Frick shrugged as if Burt Conyers was beyond the fringe of sanity. "One day I'll tell you some stories about that man," he promised.

"First tell me where Ida Day is buried!" Rose blurted out.

Harland Frick gave her a suspicious look.

"Why do you want to know that?"

She hesitated. She wanted to be honest but she didn't want to be perceived as irrational by her friend. She didn't know if he would appreciate her fears.

Finally she opted for honesty. "My friend Didi Nightingale is very smart. But she doesn't believe in the supernatural. I do, Harland. Oh yes. I *do* believe that Lubin's Field is haunted. I believe that Ida Day was a witch of some sort. Maybe a good witch . . . maybe a kind witch."

Harland sharpened his pencil point again, although the pencil had no need of it.

Rose stood up. "It may seem stupid to you, but I want to go to her grave and ask forgiveness . . . and ask her protection for my dogs."

"I understand," Harland replied. "She was cremated."

"And her ashes? Where are they?"

He tapped the pencil on the counter several times. Then he gave out with a profound sigh and laid the pencil down gently, fastidiously.

"If you cross Lubin's Field to the eastern edge, you'll find a path. That path leads to Ida's cottage. The cottage itself is gone, destroyed by fire and vandals. Follow the path around the shell of the cottage and you'll come to a small spring-fed steam. Ida used to get her water there. By a big split rock. The ashes, I understand, were strewn there. Right in the stream."

Rose kissed him on the top of his head and left the store quickly.

The two dogs in her car—Bozo and Huck—greeted her with hysterical yelps.

She ignored them and drove immediately to and onto the field. She left the car on the eastern edge, leashed the dogs, and began to search for the path.

It was not hard to find even though it was overgrown. Once on the path, she slowed, a little tentative now, a little frightened. She had the ridiculous feeling that she ought to remove her shoes, as if she were entering the precincts of some holy Tibetan shrine. But she kept her shoes on.

The dogs were strangely silent and tractable.

When she reached the foundation of the ruined cottage she slowed considerably, but she followed the path as Harland had instructed.

She passed old corroded wooden beehives. She passed two overgrown herb gardens, their stone borders chipped but intact.

And then she came to the stream. Or rather a rivulet; perhaps a foot across at its widest point. The stream seemed to vanish and reappear beneath the earth at intervals.

She stood still. A soft breeze was blowing.

Everything seemed to have become quiet. She could not hear any birds.

Huck, her Corgi, began to whine.

She saw the split rock, straddling the water, about twenty yards upstream.

She started toward it, not thinking yet of what ritual she would use to placate the witch. She stopped abruptly ten yards from the split rock.

Something was lying on the ground.

A chill went down her back. She pulled the dogs close to her.

Dr. Nightingale smiled. The big chestnut mare was standing in the far end of her stall in a reflective pose. Didi treated many horses in her practice but she never ceased to be intrigued by the way they developed poses while in their stalls. The poses were so mysterious. The horses seemed to be engaged in deep philosophical thought. Often they would raise one back leg as if the burden of deep thought was so severe it was necessary to elevate a limb to ease intellectual tension.

Didi clucked softly. Glowworm turned her beautiful head to regard the interloper.

Didi removed a lump of brown sugar from her shirt pocket, placed it prominently in her palm and thrust her hand through the slats, into the stall.

Glowworm turned slowly, her eyes on the sugar, and then ambled toward the delicacy.

The moment she reached the sugar, Didi pulled it away and moved a step along the stall. Glowworm followed. Didi moved. Glowworm followed. As she and the mare played this chase-the-sugar game, Didi studied the horse carefully.

Yes. There was no doubt the big lady was moving better. And there was no doubt the bump on her back had diminished.

Didi gave Glowworm the sugar.

"She's better, isn't she?" The voice came from behind. Didi turned and saw a smiling Lilly Donniger, still with a cane.

"Much better," Didi agreed.

Mrs. Donniger hobbled over to the stall and the two women watched Glowworm for a long while. She, in turn, seemed to be watching them for signs of more brown sugar.

Finally, Mrs. Donniger said, "I often wonder about Glowworm. When she was young. Can you imagine how beautiful she was as a three-year-old? Can you imagine when they took her out at her first hunt meeting . . . the first time she heard the foxhounds baying? Oh Lord! It must have been exquisite."

Didi nodded sympathetically. She suffered the romanticism of horse owners gladly.

"You know," Mrs. Donniger continued, "I

heard it was John Breitland himself who trained Glowworm. He was a wonderful horseman. That was before he became a recluse, of course." She caught her breath, as if the memories had suddenly become painful. "It is such a tragedy."

"You mean his murder?"

"Oh that too! But I was talking about the Hillsbrook Hunt. How we all miss it in the spring and fall. It was so lovely to see them in the distance. It was like stepping into a magical world—something out of another time and place."

Here we go again, thought Didi. Everyone seemed to have his own nostalgic take on that institution.

"A magical world," Lilly repeated, this time with such a strange fury that Didi looked intently at the old woman.

There were tears streaming down Lilly Donniger's face and she was doing something queer with her cane—pounding it into the hard dirt of the stable floor. *Thud. Thud. Thud.*

Didi yearned to console her but all she could think of was what her mother used to say: "Good memories lie."

Mrs. Donniger smiled through her tears and patted Didi's arm. "Maybe," she said, "it's the way it ended that makes everyone so sad. I mean, it was so sudden."

"Sudden? But, Mrs. Donniger, they had been running out of open land for a long time. Let's face it—Hillsbrook hasn't really been good fox hunting country since the 1970s."

"No, dear. You have it wrong. That wasn't why John Breitland closed the Hillsbrook Hunt Club down."

Didi was puzzled. "Why, then?"

"Something terrible happened," Lilly said ominously.

Didi was silent, allowing Lilly to tell the story at her own pace.

"No one knows precisely what happened," the old woman went on, "but it had something to do with John Breitland's dogs."

"What dogs?"

"The foxhounds."

Didi shrugged. This was a new wrinkle in the legend. "What happened to the foxhounds?"

"Oh, I wouldn't know. But it was something terrible."

A cryptic horror story, Didi mused. Something way out and scary—and totally undocumented. Veterinarians hear them once a week.

The talk of dogs, however, make her think of Aretha. "Remember, Mrs. Donniger—no riding Glowworm. Give her another week."

"Yes, of course," Lilly replied. She perked up then. "But I still haven't gotten your bill."

"It's in the mail," Didi lied.

Didi drove back to the house, waved to Abigail, who was playing with one of the yard dogs, and went into the clinic through its front door. The clinic could be entered through a wing of the main house as well. But using that entrance would entail a conversation with the ever talkative Mrs. Tunney and Didi simply was not up to that now.

Aretha was where she had left her that morning, on the bed of blankets that Didi and Rose had prepared for her in one corner of the office.

"Hello, girl," Didi called lovingly to the shepherd. "How are we doing?"

Aretha, stretched out on her left side, opened her big eyes and thumped her tail contentedly.

She's doing fine, Didi thought.

"Why don't you say hello to *me*, girlfriend?"

Didi turned toward the words. Rose was seated in a yoga position on the rug. The tone of her question had been almost bitter. Her face was ashen.

"I didn't see you," Didi replied. "What's the matter with you? Are you sick?"

"Yeah. With fear."

"What happened?"

"I went to Ida Day's grave. And I . . . found . . ."

"What? What?" Didi asked in alarm.

"I found something there."

"For god sakes, Rose, tell me what it is!"

"Here, look for yourself. It's on your desk."

She rushed to her desk, searching almost frantically, but could see only an innocuous-looking package, simply a few sheets of the local daily newspaper wrapped around an object.

She looked over at Rose in puzzlement.

"Open it, Didi."

She did so. Inside the papers were some kind of flowers—not dried but long past their prime. Long, thin stalks with several many-petaled flowers at the tip of each. They were paper-white narcissus that had been removed from the onionlike bulbs from which they sprouted.

"Look at the newspapers," Rose ordered, her voice very close to hysteria.

Didi spread the newsprint sheets out. The date printed at the top of each page was the day after the John Breitland murder.

"What does it mean, Didi?" Rose asked, almost imploring.

"I don't know," she answered quietly.

Without warning, Rose exploded. "You don't know! You always seem to know everything. But now, when I need you, you know from nothing."

Didi was silent.

"I'm sorry . . . I'm sorry for shouting, Didi. I didn't mean it. But I'm so scared now."

Didi sat down behind the desk and stared at the withered bouquet.

An old and familiar feeling began to wash over her, but it was hardly a comforting sensation. She had begun to feel like a frightened child lost in her mother's pine forest—cold, helpless.

"Who told you where the grave was?" Didi asked.

"Harland."

"Yes, I should have known. Why did you go there?"

"To ask her for help. To commune with her spirit. To ask her to protect Aretha and the others . . . I don't know."

"Rose," Didi said sternly, "it's time you took me to Harland Frick."

Chapter 5

"Where have you been?" Wynton Chung asked as Allie Voegler slipped into the passenger side of the car and grabbed the binoculars out of Chung's hands.

"Brooding," Allie said.

"I've been trying to contact you for an hour," Chung complained.

Allie raised the glasses to his eyes and stared straight ahead while he answered the young officer. "A scab fell off an old wound. You know what that's like, right? I had to look at that wound again after all these years."

"I have no idea what you're talking about, Allie."

"That's good! Now, what's up?"

"The hogs are rooting."

"Say what?"

Chung laughed. "Just trying to pick up some farm country lingo."

"Hillsbrook's dairy country, not farm country."

"Six of one, half a dozen of the other," Chung

noted lazily. "But take a look. Just to the right of the entrance."

Allie adjusted the focus knob on the binoculars. It was a bit difficult to see because the late-afternoon sun was flooding the horizon.

The pickup truck with the new radial tires had been pulled around front. Sonny James and his girlfriend Paula were furiously kicking through the junk and debris that circled their large tent. They appeared to be a bit drunk, alternating between singing and laughing. And every once in a while they flung something into a large carton in the bed of the pickup.

"Spring cleaning?" Chung asked.

"Looks like. But who knows?"

"What are they throwing into the truck, Allie?"

"I can't see."

"I don't think it's anything incriminating. But I figured you ought to know."

"You figured right."

"I mean, Allie, Sonny is a loose cannon. It damn well might be cut-up snow tires and disassembled murder weapons."

"Anything's possible."

Paula and Sonny began to dance amidst the junk.

"At least they're enjoying themselves," Chung quipped. "They look like a real happy couple."

"So it seems, so it seems."

Then Sonny and the girl went back into the tent.

"What now?" Chung asked.

"You were the one who got me here. What do you think?"

"I think we wait. I think something's going down."

Allie laughed. Chung always hit you with a bundle of ridiculous metaphors. First it was "the hogs are rooting." Then it was his appropriation of NYPD slang—"something's going down."

"Did the connection ever get firmed up, Allie?"

"What connection?"

"Sonny James and Orin Rafael. Is it documented?"

"Well, we know they knew each other. Sonny did hauling for him at different times."

"What kind?"

"Feed in, manure out. From Rafael's boarding stable."

"How much do you think Rafael paid Sonny?"

"For the hauling?"

"No, for the hit."

"I don't know."

"Well, take a guess. I mean, was it five hundred? Five thousand? Fifty thousand?"

"I don't know. We had a case up here about five years ago. Right here on the Ridge. A guy named Tom Drabble paid a drifter sixty-six bucks and a bottle of Wild Turkey to kill his wife."

"But Breitland wasn't trailer park trash."

"Ain't that the truth," Allie affirmed.

Suddenly people appeared outside of the tent again. She headed toward the pickup, then stopped and turned back and began to curse Sonny James with a vile and imaginative chain of expletives. Finally she climbed into the truck and took off.

Allie got quickly out of the car. "You stick with Sonny," he ordered Chung. "I'll see what she's up to."

He followed the pickup at a distance of about five hundred feet. It didn't take him long to realize Paula was drunk; she was weaving a bit and driving a little too fast. And she had not turned her lights on even though darkness had fallen.

Actually, driving at night without lights was not so uncommon a thing in Hillsbrook. It was a part of the folk wisdom that driving with no lights in the early evening is the way to avoid hitting deer, since deer become transfixed by headlights and just stand waiting to be hit. There was some truth to the belief.

Paula's vehicle was still clearly visible because of the flickering red rear brake lights.

Allie was tempted to pull her over and write up a DWI citation. But he refrained. He was after bigger game.

The girl wasn't going to the Hillsbrook town dump as he had guessed. She turned off half a mile before the dump and headed north. Once outside the village limits she turned on the headlights and increased her speed.

Twenty minutes later she pulled up at the English Springs town dump. It was the same physically as the one in Hillsbrook—a hole in the earth with a graded ramp for trucks. Most people just flung their bags into the pit and drove away.

Like the Hillsbrook dump, it had a new, most impressive sign detailing dumping procedures. Recycling had come to Dutchess County. Glass and metal required one color bag, regular trash another. Different color bags were to be thrown in different areas of the pit. Newspapers had to be placed in large bins outside the pit.

Allie could see Paula reading the sign carefully. The entrance to the dump was brightly illuminated by floodlights.

Paula seemed to find the instructions amusing. But she soon became infuriated. She cursed the sign, went back to the truck, and unloaded two cartons.

From the front seat of the pickup she brought out three large black plastic sacks. Then she transferred the contents of the cartons and closed the bags with string. Then she flung the empty cartons into the pit. With difficulty, she dragged the bags to the edge of the pit and flung them over the top. When that was finished she did a little hopping dance at the lip of the pit.

Allie could see her face clearly. She was a handsome freckled woman of about thirty. Her hair was brownish red. She was muscular, as if she had handled horses for many years, and in fact she was dressed like a rodeo cowboy, down to the bandanna around her neck. Very attractive, Allie thought. But what the hell was she doing driving all this way to dump garbage? There were only two possibilities. One, she didn't want to use the dump in Hillsbrook for reasons of secrecy. Two, she was just angry at Sonny and wanted to take a long drive. As for the secrecy angle—that was stretching the point a bit. No one sifted through garbage in the Hillsbrook facility. At least, not that he knew of. And if something was to be hidden, why dump it at all? Was the murder weapon in one of those bags? Not likely. What about a piece of a disassembled weapon? Perhaps. What about the snow tires? But why not just burn them?

Allie didn't know what to make of the situation. But when Paula drove off, he climbed out of his car and meandered down the ramp and into the pit.

Using a penknife, he slit open the first of the three bags Paula had dumped.

It was obvious that she had not followed instructions as to bag color. The black bag was filled with empty whiskey bottles and beer cans. There was also a burned-out toaster and dozens of old *Hot Rod* magazines.

He slit open the second bag.

More empties. Old frayed electrical cords. Broken metal ice cube trays. An old lamp. Several splintered broom and mop handles.

He picked up the lamp. It was kind of pretty. Like the ones he had to make in shop classes at school. This one had a thin mesh as the lamp shade; the lamp looked like a lady at a funeral, a lady wearing a veil. But the wiring and the base had corroded. He dropped it back down. He picked up two of the ice cube trays. Their edges looked singed, as if they had been rescued from a fire. Well, so what? He abandoned them, too.

Then he opened the third bag. Rubber treads! Excited, he knelt beside the bag and separated the rubber strips from the rest of the trash.

But no, these weren't fragments of snow tires. They were old bicycle tires without tubes.

Allie stood upright then, suddenly weary and feeling very stupid. Look at what he was doing: mucking around in some reeking pit in the dark, up to his ankles in garbage.

"Charlie! What are you doing here at this hour?"

Blanche Hopper was genuinely surprised and, it seemed, genuinely pleased to see her cousin standing in the doorway of her little cottage. "Who would have thought you'd be dropping by again so soon? I don't see you for ages and ages, and they suddenly you're here twice in a—"

"Something kind of important's come up, Blanche. So I asked Trent Tucker here to drive me over."

"Well, come on in then. By all means, come on in."

Charlie walked inside. The first thing he saw was Yam, who was crouched in the kitchen eating his dinner. He looked up at Charlie with great suspicion, but he never stopped eating.

"Sit, Charlie, sit," Blanche urged. "As soon as Yam finishes his dinner I'll make some coffee."

"Won't be necessary, Blanche. I have to talk and go."

"Talk then."

"Well, Blanche," he began, sitting down gingerly, "here's the thing. There used to be a program on the televisions about a veterinarian over in England."

"There were two of them, Charlie," Blanche corrected him. "I remember the shows well."

"It was called *All Things Wise and Happy*."

"No, Charlie. I think it was *All Things Brave and Tall*."

"No, no. Wait . . . It was more like *All Things Big and Little*, I think. Anyway, it doesn't matter. But the important thing is that a television producer in Albany wants to make another veterinarian thing for the television."

"That's nice," Blanche said. "I watched only a few of them, but they were nice. They were always helping cows give birth and then celebrating in a pub."

"That's right, Blanche. Well, this one won't take place in England. And it'll be about a real live vet."

He leaned forward as if he were about to disclose some extremely secretive and highly important information.

"It'll be about Dr. Didi Quinn Nightingale."

"My!" was all Blanche could get out.

"Yup. It's going to be several days in the life of a real country vet."

"Are you going to be in it, Charlie?"

"I suppose I will," he admitted, modesty itself. He then looked over at the yellow cat who had finished his food and was now cleaning up his whiskers. Charlie shifted his weight in the chair. This was going to be one of the tallest tales he had ever spun. The cat eyed him keenly. Yam seemed to be grinning. But then he sauntered into his bedroom without so much as a backward glance at the interloper.

"Is there something bothering you?" Blanche asked.

Charlie didn't like her tone. He had to reassert control over the situation.

"Let me be honest, Blanche. Real honest. The producer, the man in charge of this whole TV thing, is a fool. I mean a real fool. And he says that he loves everything about the series, so far, except the fact that Miss Quinn don't have a pet."

"I don't understand."

"It's like this, Blanche. We got horses, pigs, dogs, and cats in all the buildings on the Nightingale property—except the main house. There's all kinds of animals just *outside* the house but no animals *inside*."

"Isn't that strange?"

"That's what the producer said, Blanche. He said Miss Quinn has to have a . . . how did he put it . . . a nonhuman confidant."

"What?"

"A confidant. Nonhuman."

"Well, that makes sense, I guess."

"He said Miss Quinn needs a cat for her clinic. He said a dog would be okay also, but he liked a cat best. There could be scenes . . . beautiful scenes. Miss Quinn in the clinic office late at night, looking through her microscope at some kind of lice or flea eggs that she scraped out of a goat's ear. She is tired. She's lonely. And in comes her precious little cat to console her."

"Oh, that is beautiful!" Blanche said.

"Yes, but she don't have a cat—see?"

"She could bring in one of the barn cats."

"That's right. She could do that. But I have a better idea."

"What's that?"

"Yam!"

"Yam?"

"Yes. He'll be part of the cast, see? He plays Miss Quinn's beloved cat. He's smart and he's handsome and, as you say, he's a lovable pussy cat. Can't you just see it, Blanche? The whole country will fall in love with Yam. Maybe even he'll get his own show."

Blanche laughed nervously. She was obviously struck by the idea. But she was frightened.

"It will be easy, Blanche. You don't have to do anything. Not a thing. I'll pick Yam up, like tomorrow evening. I'll take him over there. They do the filming late at night and early in the morning. Then I'll bring him back to you. He won't be gone for more than twelve hours at a time. Maybe three or four nights a week."

"It takes my breath away, Charlie. Just think of it. Yam, a television star!"

"Wouldn't Al feel good if he was here?" Charlie said.

"Yes, he would."

"Why sure, he would. He's going to be chuckling in his grave."

"Everybody loves Yam," Blanche said dreamily.

"Oh that is the truth, Blanche. He's one cat in a million, that Yam."

"Do you think I should tell him now, Charlie?"

"Tell who?"

"Yam of course. He's in his room."

"By all means," Charlie said, standing up. "You go in there and give him the news. But I have to go now. I'll be by tomorrow night."

Blanche saw him out, slamming the door behind him and then rushing into the small room just past the kitchen where Yam lay sleeping. What good news she had to share.

Charlie walked very slowly toward Trent Tucker's vehicle. He was pleased . . . almost, in fact, bordering on the ecstatic, no mean feat for a man his age. Everything was on schedule. Everything was falling into place. Wyatt Earp would soon emerge. And the world of field mice would never be the same. Charlie chuckled.

"I don't like the way you're talking to me," an irate Harland Frick said to Didi.

The health food store was closed. The blinds were drawn.

Rose came to her friend's defense. "She means no harm, Harland. We're just all frightened."

"Not frightened enough to be stupid," Didi said.

"Then let me say it again. Rose was the only one who I told where Ida Day's grave was. But Rose was the only one who asked me. In fact, she's the only one who ever asked me anything about Ida Day."

"And this?" Didi asked, pointing to the strange bouquet Rose had found near Ida Day's grave.

"What about it?" Harland said testily.

"Do you know anything about it? Do you have any idea who put it there? And why?"

"Not a clue," he said, turning the flowers over and over in his hands and fingering the withered remains of the petals.

"You do see the date on that newspaper, don't you? It's the day after Breitland was murdered."

"I see it," Frick answered.

"Tell me, Harland, do you really think Ida Day was a witch?"

Rose broke in. "He never said she was a witch, Didi. That was my idea. And you really don't know what you're saying. I'm not claiming the old woman was one of those broomstick witches. She wasn't a Halloween cutout. I'm talking about something else. I'm *not* talking about sitting around a campfire with two other cackling crones."

"What kind of witch was she then?" Didi asked impatiently.

"It's hard to say. For me, a witch is a woman who knows secrets; who knows the rhythms of the land; who knows the secret things. Yes. Maybe that's it. The secret things."

"Make some sense, Rose," Didi said.

"Oh, Didi, you know what I mean. You know very well what I'm talking about."

Didi turned to Harland Frick. "Is Rose right? Did Ida know 'secret things'?"

"She was an old woman when she died. She kept bees and grew medicinal herbs. I don't know what kind of secrets she knew, if any."

"Did people consult her?"

"Consult? You mean like a fortune-teller?"

"Yes."

"Not that I know. A few people went to Ida when they had a headache. She'd make tea for you."

"Did she have any close friends?"

"How should I know?"

"Well, somebody buried her ashes, Harland."

"To tell the truth, I can't exactly be sure that's her grave site. It's just what I heard—somewhere."

"What about a husband? Or children? Or a lover?"

"No, none. Look, months could go by and nobody would see her. She was a recluse for many years."

"So was John Breitland," Didi snapped. "And look what happened to him."

She fell silent for a long time after that comment. She wasn't even sure what she had meant by the remark. She heard Rose and Harland whispering to each other. Good. They deserved each other. Nature Girl meets Thoreau. Didi wandered down the row of organic chips. And then into the small dairy section filled with goat milk products. She picked up a small round of cheese and checked the price. It was frightfully expensive. She played with it in her hands. Her interchange with Harland Frick had been a bit disrespectful, she knew. But there was something about him that had always bothered her. It was hard to pin down. Oh, there was no doubt that he knew more about Hillsbrook than anyone else knew—or cared to know. But he never seemed to know any hard facts. It was always allusion and maybes and generalizations with a little homespun wisdom and a few old local legends mixed in. And he never ever disclosed his sources, so sometimes you began to wonder if Harland was as crazy as some of the eccentrics he talked about.

She dropped the cheese back into the open freezer. Then she turned the corner, walked back down another aisle and ended up where she had started. Harland was peeling an organic tangerine. Rose had her eyes closed and seemed to be humming some strange melody.

Didi asked, "Was Ida Day born in Hillsbrook?"

"Born and bred," Harland replied.

"And her family had been in the area a long time, I assume."

"Yes. Since about 1791. They came down from the North during some Indian trouble."

"You said 1791?"

"So I hear."

"Did they farm?"

"No. I hear they originally were candle makers. Then lawyers. Two of the Day sons died at Gettysburg. I guess they were Ida's uncles."

"Or great-uncles," Rose interjected.

"What did Ida look like?" Didi asked.

"Well . . . I guess you could say she looked like a lot of old ladies look."

"No, I mean when she was younger. Do you know of any pictures of her as a young woman?"

Harland shook his head.

"There probably are photos of her somewhere. She did know a lot of people."

"Wait a minute, Harland! I thought you said she was a recluse."

"Yes, I did. I did. But that was later on. I mean, she did everything that people did to survive in Hillsbrook during bad times. The Days weren't rich. They worked in the factory just like I did, and a thousand others."

Didi tensed. This story was getting mighty peculiar. First, Ida Day was some kind of earth mother. Now she's working in a factory.

"What factory are you talking about, Harland?"

"You know. The Breitland factory."

Didi exhaled. It might turn out not to be especially significant, but the Breitland factory was the first concrete connection to emerge between Ida Day and the late John Breitland.

"Sooner or later," Harland said, "everybody ended up working at the factory. Charlie Gravis worked there a few months in the sixties. I wager you never knew that. And your Mrs. Tunney. Even crazy Burt Conyers. Even our lady mayor, when she was no more than a girl. Remember, the place didn't shut down till the midseventies."

Harland seemed to become wistful. "That factory made the best farm implements in the country."

He would have talked more, but Rose was becoming impatient. "Aretha, Didi," she said. "You promised to help me get Aretha back to my place this evening."

"Right. We'll go now."

They said good-bye to Harland and together walked out to the jeep.

"I fixed her up a place in the barn where she won't get a chill," Rose said.

Didi didn't respond. She was staring straight ahead, her eyes on the road.

Then, without warning, she pulled the car onto the shoulder of the road and braked sharply.

Rose regarded her warily. "What are you stopping here for?"

"Take a look."

"At what?"

"At that house," Didi said, nodding in the direction of a large place set back off the road.

"Whose place is that?"

"John Breitland's," said Didi. She shut the engine then.

"Yeah . . . so? It's just a house, isn't it?"

Didi struck the steering wheel with a fist. "I just had the sudden notion that we ought to go inside."

"Why?" There was suspicion in Rose's eyes as well as her words.

"I don't really know."

"What do you think you're going to find in there, Dr. Night Gown?"

"I said I don't know."

Rose hunched over in her seat.

"Besides," she added, "it would be illegal to go in there, right? We'd be breaking and entering . . . right?"

"Yes," Didi said simply.

Rose clasped her hands as if in prayer. "And it could be dangerous," she said.

"How so?"

Rose laughed nervously, her voice escalating into a high register. "Look, Didi. We could go in there and there could be some kind of apparition waiting for us."

"What do you mean—Ida Day?"

"Yes! She could be waiting for us in a chair, holding a bouquet of dead paper-whites wrapped in a newspaper that reports her murder."

"Oh, Rose, please. You're going off the deep end."

"That's what living is about, Didi."

Didi sat back. The house was looming before them. She had no idea why she had stopped at Breitland's house. It was just there and she knew only that she had to stop there. And now that she had stopped, the house was exerting some sort of pull on her. She wanted to go in there. Now. There was no rational explanation. It was like a lighthouse on a foggy night. One sailed toward it, one tied the ship up to it. Yes, a lighthouse.

Didi climbed out of the jeep. Rose went after her, however reluctantly. They followed the road for a bit, then cut across the field to avoid the driveway.

"Lo, we have become criminals," Rose announced melodramatically.

They climbed the steps. The front door was locked. They circled the house along the wrap-around porch, trying each window. The place was locked down.

"We could just smash a window," Rose suggested.

"I don't want to do that," Didi replied.

"In for a penny, in for a pound," the other warned.

The root cellar in the back of the house was also bolted. Didi went back to the jeep and returned with a flashlight. The two women fought with the mildewed latch on the cellar door for five minutes. It finally fell apart.

They swung the wooden slat doors open and descended. The cellar was empty. But a dull red door at the far end opened onto a small staircase, and then into the pantry.

Once in the house, Didi closed all the shutters and flicked on all the lights.

It was a dumbfounding scene.

The house was virtually bare of everything that would constitute a normal dwelling: rugs, chairs, tables, photographs, paintings, knick-knacks.

There was one chair in the living room. And one table. There was one small bed in each of the bedrooms. There was one table in the kitchen and the barest minimum of utensils.

"He was more than a recluse," Rose said. "He was almost a monk. I once heard about a monastery in Ireland where the monks sleep in the coffins that will be used to bury them."

Didi sat down on the single living room chair.

She stared at what seemed to have been John Breitland's only indulgence: a magnificent hi-fi system and three huge piles of old-fashioned vinyl opera records. She stared at the blank walls.

She was profoundly disturbed—by one thing in particular. It was the first living space she had ever entered in which the inhabitant was a passionate horseman and didn't have a single photograph, trophy, or memento displayed. The lack of such items was even more dramatic in Breitland's case. This wasn't just any old equestrian. This was the man whose whole life seemed to have been dedicated to the Hillsbrook Hunt Club until it was shut down.

Didi sat in silence for another few minutes while Rose looked through the records. Then they opened the shutters, put the lights out, and slipped out the way they had come in.

As they drove off, Rose said, "I didn't feel Ida Day's presence at all there."

Chapter 6

Mrs. Tunney was making the oatmeal, as always, in a large cast-iron pot, stirring it slowly with a long wooden spoon.

The sugar, butter, and milk were on the table. The toast, fresh from the toaster, was being buttered by Trent Tucker and passed around to Charlie Gravis and Abigail.

The coffeepot was on the table. But not a drop would be poured until Mrs. Tunney finished the oatmeal, portioned it out into bowls, distributed it, and took her place at the table.

The morning was beautiful. Spring at its most glorious. Old Mrs. Tunney hummed a bit as she spooned the oats from pot to bowl.

Just as she was transporting the now full bowls to the table, she looked through the screen door and saw, to her consternation, that Didi was not in her usual place in the backyard doing her usual set of strange exercises.

In fact, the young doctor was nowhere to be seen.

"Miss Quinn isn't down yet. That's not like

her," Mrs. Tunney said in a worried tone as she pulled out her chair and the others fell upon their cereal.

"Everybody has a right to sleep late once in a while," Charlie said. He was feeling very kindly toward the world and everyone in it lately.

"It's only six-fifteen," Trent Tucker noted.

"She's always up by now," Mrs. Tunney insisted. "Up and dressed and doing those fool exercises out there. Breathing in and breathing out . . . in and out. Sometimes I think—"

She suddenly stopped, as if she were about to say something she might regret later on. She played with the oatmeal in her bowl. The others were eating with gusto.

"Something's worrying the Miss," she finally said.

Trent Tucker burst out laughing. Tunney's frown squelched the laughter, though.

"I'd be worried, too," Trent said, "if someone put a bullet through my friend's dog."

"Wait! I hear something!" the old housekeeper said urgently. "She must be getting up now."

"I don't hear nothing," Charlie responded.

"You don't hear your own footsteps, Gravis," she snapped nastily. Mrs. Tunney turned to Abigail then. "You must have heard her, didn't you?"

Mrs. Tunney was always asking questions of Abigail but rarely got an answer. Abigail, in this case, only smiled and continued with the elaborate brown sugar design she was building in her bowl.

Mrs. Tunney's hearing processes were confirmed a few moments later when it was obvious that someone was descending the stairs from the second-floor bedroom and that that someone was Deirdre Quinn Nightingale.

Didi walked right into the kitchen, said good morning, as she usually did—and then did something she never did. She took some of her elves' toast and coffee. And she stood right next to where Mrs. Tunney sat as she did so.

No one at the table knew what to do. It was a definite breach of tradition.

Didi finished the piece of toast . . . drained the coffee . . . and said with a flourish, "I'm not doing yoga this morning. I'm going to take Promise Me for a ride."

She walked out of the kitchen door. Everyone at the table exchanged glances. Yes, no doubt Mrs. Tunney had been right again. Something was bothering Miss Quinn. She was acting a bit strangely.

After the oatmeal and toast, Mrs. Tunney asked if anyone wanted eggs. No one did, except for Abigail, who asked for one poached egg. Mrs. Tunney made it gladly. Trent Tucker went off to do some chores.

Charlie Gravis walked outside and stood right where Didi usually did her yoga exercises.

He squinted across the fields, into the pine forest. He caught a speck of white tail. But this was to be expected. The deer always came through the pine forest in the spring—to drink at the Nightingale ponds.

Then he saw Didi leading Promise Me out of the barn. The big bay thoroughbred was all tacked up and looked raring to go.

Didi was talking to the horse and rubbing his nose, then she lightly climbed aboard.

Charlie grinned. It was nice seeing young people move so quickly, so effortlessly. It had been so long since he had been able to climb on a horse like that, he couldn't even remember the approximate year or the approximate horse.

Miss Quinn thought he knew nothing about horses. She was right. But he sure as hell had known how to ride them. And he knew what he liked and disliked.

He watched Didi guide Promise Me into the field at a walk.

What a beautiful animal that Promise Me was. But Charlie never would buy a thoroughbred. Their legs were too long and thin—like matchsticks. They made him nervous.

When the money started rolling in from his pied piper scheme he sure was going to buy a horse—maybe a few of them. But not thoroughbreds. Oh no. He liked Morgans. He liked the way they set up and the way they moved. Yep, a black Morgan filly.

Charlie saw Didi move Promise Me into a trot.

Then it happened.

Two rabbits came from nowhere and darted under the big horse's front hooves.

Promise Me shied to the left suddenly and pulled up.

Didi flew over the horse's right shoulder.

"Mrs. Tunney!" Charlie yelled and then shuffled out onto the field as fast as he could.

When he reached the scene of the accident, Promise Me was grazing happily about twenty feet from Didi. She was sitting up on the ground, her head between her hands.

"Are you okay?" Charlie asked.

She nodded affirmatively.

"Don't get up yet!" he ordered. Didi lifted her head and waved with one hand to let him know she knew the drill. Then she began to rub her hands down her limbs to make sure everything was intact.

Within minutes, all Didi's elves were around her. Mrs. Tunney was frantic with worry, screaming about the dangers of horse riding. But Trent Tucker had gathered Promise Me's reins and Abigail was smiling sweetly, as if this were exactly what should happen on a beautiful spring morning in the country.

Didi held out a hand. Charlie grasped it and pulled her up. "Well," he quipped, "at least you won't need a cane like Mrs. Donniger."

He was about to make another quip when he saw that her face was ashen and there was a funny look in her eyes. "Do you want to sit back down again, Doc?" he asked, still holding her hand tightly.

"No. I'm fine," she said. But the young doctor didn't seem fine to Charlie. She was looking around wildly.

"I saw it when I was falling," she said.

"You mean the rabbits?" Charlie asked. "There were two of them. They just flew out of their holes under your horse's nose."

"Not the rabbits!"

"What then?"

"The video, Charlie, the video!"

He stared dumbly at her. Charlie didn't have the slightest idea what young Dr. Nightingale was talking about.

Five minutes after he walked out of the store, Allie Voegler was unhappy with his purchase—a ham and cheese sandwich on a roll. What he really wanted was egg salad.

It was that contradiction he was exploring in his head when he climbed the stairs of the building that housed the Hillsbrook Police Department. His small office was on the second floor.

Why, in fact, had he gone into the store to purchase an egg salad on white and ended up with ham and cheese on a roll?

Then he saw Deirdre Quinn Nightingale waiting in front of his office door.

Allie froze. It was a moment of panic. Was she going to bring up that old murder again? Was she going to goad him into admitting that ever since that kid Mosely died in prison the case had been a canker on his conscience? He had done the right thing. He had gone by the book. By all the yardsticks, the kid was guilty as sin. But still . . .

Then he saw that Didi did not look well. Something had happened to her!

Allie forgot about himself, closed the gap between them quickly, took her by the arm, and led her quickly into his office.

He took his usual seat behind the desk and dropped the bag with his sandwich onto the desk. She took the chair opposite his. Allie reached out for her instinctively. She accepted the hand he proffered and for a moment, just for a moment, took it into her own hand, but then pulled back.

"I guess I look pretty bad," she said.

"You look like something happened."

"Promise Me threw me. Just a few hours ago."

"Anything broken? Inside or out."

"No. I'm fine." She laughed bitterly. "No, I'm really not fine, Allie. I want to see that video again."

"Video?"

"The one of the Breitland murder."

"Hell, you must have seen it a million times. I know I have. Everybody has. They play it morning, noon, and night on TV."

"I know, I know, Allie. I want to see it in slow motion though, and I want to see it with you."

"Are you asking me out on a movie date? Popcorn; necking in the balcony; all that stuff?"

His joke went flat. Didi's face remained impassive.

"Okay, Didi. What's going on?"

"You'll see. Can you play that video now?"

"Here?"

"Yes. Here."

"I don't have a copy of it. Why don't you just wait until it comes on again? Sit down, turn on your TV set, and wait. Sooner or later it'll be on again."

"There's no time, Allie. Can you take me over to the TV station?"

"No. The chief has issued a no-fraternization order. We don't talk to those TV people anymore. They promised us they wouldn't reveal that Orin Rafael was our number-one suspect. Then they told the world."

"It's very important that we see that video—now, together," Didi persisted.

"Why? Why is it so important? What's going on, Didi? Did that fall rattle your brains or something?"

She did not reply. She sat back and closed her eyes.

I would love to hold her, he thought. I wish I could kiss that spot on the back of her neck.

She opened her eyes then. "You have the wrong man, Allie," she said quietly.

He laughed in derision. "The wrong man? What wrong man? No one has been charged yet in the Breitland killing. We don't have any man at all."

"You misunderstand."

"What is there to misunderstand?"

"I meant the wrong man was murdered."

Allie sat upright in his chair. He didn't know yet what Didi was saying, but something told him to take her seriously, to stop the wisecracks and the teasing and ask no further questions for the moment. The truth was, he *could* get the tape quickly. He knew, in fact, who had shot the video. It was Jim Bartolo, the host of a local radio show on WKDF.FM. Bartolo came on every evening at seven and gave a rundown of all social and cultural events in the Hillsbrook area that would take place in the next forty-eight hours. And he gave snippets of local news and took calls from listeners.

Bartolo had been in Lubin's Field that day, with his sheepdog Adolphus. He had been there to get Adolphus blessed. And he was videotaping the proceedings for his own enjoyment. It was Bartolo who had sold the video to the TV station. Yes, Allie had quick access to the master tape, if he wanted it.

"Well?" Didi pressed.

Allie hesitated only a few seconds more. Then he got the dispatcher on the intercom and obtained Bartolo's home phone number.

He dialed the number. Bartolo answered on the fourth ring. It was obvious he had been sleeping.

"It's Allie Voegler, Jim."

"What do you want at this hour?"

"It's about noon."

"That's what I mean."

"I need to take a peek at your video," Allie said.

"You mean my great film noir—*Splattered Brains*?"

"Yeah. I need to look at it now."

"Sure. Come on over."

"I'm bringing a friend."

"Is she good looking?"

"Does a cow give milk?"

Bartolo hung up. Allie turned to Didi. "We'll take your jeep," he said, "so I can eat some lunch on the way over."

They reached Bartolo's place in ten minutes. Allie didn't finish his sandwich. The radio host lived in one of the first housing developments built in the Hillsbrook area. Ugly, California-style split-level homes set in a serpentine pattern along a steep hill. Subsequent developments, of which there were many, tried to mimic the indigenous architecture of Hillsbrook—aptly called dairy farm Gothic.

Bartolo answered the door in his bathrobe, greeting them warmly. Adolphus, his dog, poked his head through his master's bare legs, but he soon decided that the visitors were of no interest and he soon resumed his afternoon nap.

Bartolo was a short stocky man with a beautiful deep voice. "I don't usually receive visitors at this hour," he noted.

"Do you sleep all day?" asked Allie.

"Of course. Right up to an hour before my show. Then I go to work. Then I party all night."

Didi found that funny. "Party? In Hillsbrook?"

He laughed along with her. "Ah, you country bumpkins. You don't realize it's all in the mind."

He led them down one level into a den with a

huge Sony color TV and the requisite VCR. He slapped the remote control into Allie's hand.

"It's all yours, Voegler. Just let yourself out when you're finished. And it was very nice meeting you, Dr. Nightingale. The next time Adolphus gets into difficulty I'll consult you." He walked into his bedroom and closed the door behind him.

"Play it through from beginning to end first," Didi instructed Allie when they were alone.

They sat in silence and watched the complete video.

"Play it again, Allie."

He rewound the tape and punched the Play button. This time, however, when the tape reached the point at which the bullet has entered Breitland's skull, Didi called out "Stop!"

Allie froze the tape.

"Now go back a few frames," she commanded.

He did so. Didi rose from her seat and approached the set. When she was up close to the screen she squatted in front of it, as if she were about to attack the set.

"All right, Allie," she said over her shoulder. "Go forward again—but in slow motion."

The familiar frames moved forward again. There was the wooden stage. There was Conyers, the poet. There was Breitland.

"Stop! Stop!" she shouted. Then she jumped up and ran to Allie's side. "Did you see it?"

Allie was confused by her crazy behavior. Didi had begun to babble: "I knew it! I knew it! I knew I was right. It came to me when I was falling. Like a vision. But it wasn't a vision. It was Promise Me telling me something." She raised her two fists in triumph and then, for the first time, noticed Allie's bewilderment.

"Didn't you see it?" she asked him, a bit calmer now.

"See what?"

"The poet—shying. Just like Promise Me. That's what Burt Conyers did. He shied, a second before the shot rang out. Didn't you see the movement of his head and shoulders? Not a whole lot, mind you. But enough."

Allie rewound the tape and played it through again.

"You're right," he admitted.

"Do you know why Burt shied?" she asked.

"No."

"Because a few moments before I was attacked by a beagle."

"Come again?"

"Yes, yes, a beagle, Allie. A dog who hates me. His name's Carswell. He came running at me full speed. But Abigail was watching the whole thing and she let one of the yard dogs loose to intercept Carswell. They met in one ferocious snarl. That is what Burt Conyers heard. That's why he shied."

"Okay. That much makes sense."

"The whole thing makes sense. The bullet that killed John Breitland was really meant for Burt Conyers."

"Just a minute, Didi," he said sternly. "That's jumping the gun."

"No, it isn't, Allie. Are you blind? You saw that video. The bullet was meant for Burt."

"You can't get to that conclusion from watching something done with a handheld video camera. Not unless you do all kinds of sophisticated computer analyses of the tape. And of the trajectory of the bullet. And the time factor. I mean, you're dealing with microseconds here, Didi."

Didi was silent. She stared at the now blank television screen. Finally, she said quietly, "I spoke to Harland Frick. He told me Burt once worked in the Breitland factory."

"From what I hear, a lot of people did," Allie replied.

"Ida Day also worked in the factory. Did you know that, Allie?"

He scowled at the reference to Ida Day. "Who would take a shot at Burt Conyers, Didi? I mean, who the hell would want to kill somebody like that? Can you tell me that? Is his poetry that bad? Or are you working up one of those wild conspiracy theories in your head? Ida Day, Burt Conyers, John Breitland, and . . . who? Who else are you going to throw into the pot this time?"

She made no reply. Instead, she held up the keys to the jeep and shook them noisily, then headed for the apartment door. Allie followed her outside, calling out his thanks to Jim Bartolo and slamming the door shut behind him. Bartolo apparently had gone back to sleep. When Allie looked back, he could see Adolphus's head in the bedroom window.

Allie talked all the way back into town—about ham and cheese sandwiches; about jumping to conclusions; about the distortions of videotape; and any number of other things. She was paying little or no attention to his ramblings. The intrusion of the eccentric poet Conyers in the strange web had evoked a memory in her. The memory of a poem. No, not the poem Burt was reciting to the crowd in Lubin's Field.

It was the other poem that she was thinking of. The one he was reciting one night, drunk, to no one in particular, as he stood alone in the field. The poem he had given to Abigail. And Abigail had passed it on to Didi.

As the red jeep pulled up in front of police headquarters Didi remembered exactly where that poem was: in the pages of the T.H. White book she had been reading.

"What are you going to do?" Allie said suddenly.

"The question is," Didi said grimly, "what are *you* going to do?"

Allie climbed out of the car, crunching up his sandwich bag.

"Tell me," he said bitterly, "is it really my fault that every time we get together lately it ends in some kind of fight . . . some kind of accusation . . . some kind of mistrust. Is that really my fault?"

"The fault, dear Brutus—"

Allie cut off her witty retort by whispering a scatological curse on Shakespeare and anyone who quotes him. Didi slapped him. The main force of the blow missed his face and her hand struck the door housing. It hurt.

She drove off. She drove fast. She parked haphazardly when she reached the house and ran up the stairs and into the bedroom.

Her heart sank when she noticed the pristine state of the room.

Mrs. Tunney! Mrs. Tunney had just finished cleaning the bedroom, and that meant all loose papers of any kind had been gathered and disposed of, along with everything else—animal, vegetable, or mineral—the rigorous housekeeper felt did not belong in the room.

All the books and magazines from the floor and the chairs had been stacked. Didi rushed to the bookcase and searched. Yes! There it was, on the second shelf, reshelved by Mrs. Tunney. She pulled out *The Elephant and the Kangaroo* and shook the book like a terrier with his favorite bone.

But nothing came out! She expected to see a thin sheet of paper flutter from the book's interior onto the floor. But there was nothing. The poem had probably slipped out of the book and Mrs. Tunney had trashed it.

Didi sat down on the rocker. She couldn't remember the poem in its entirety—only snippets of it. Only the last couple of lines.

Something like—"if you touch my lips I will give you either nectar or death."

That was close, she knew. Not exact, but close. When she had first read the lines, she liked them very much. In one sense they had seemed familiar. Maybe because of the imagery. Maybe because of the words themselves.

Had the poet been talking about a wild-flower? Or perhaps a Venus flytrap? One gives nectar. The other deals in death. At Lubin's Field, just before the blessing and the murder, Burt Conyers had recited a poem about wild-flowers as harbingers of death.

But no, this nectar/death couplet wasn't about a flower.

Was it simply that Conyers knew someone was going to try and murder him? After all, the poem Conyers gave Abigail was ripped from a book published before the Breitland murder in Lubin's Field.

Was it a predictive poem? No, she didn't think so. She began to rock faster in her chair. Why was the couplet familiar to her? What did it describe? Why was it obsessing her?

Didi kept on rocking. She had the feeling that those lines described something living, something in the natural world; something she had once read about.

She stood up and walked slowly to her bookcase, searching out the section that contained the books on veterinary medicine, natural history, and allied topics.

Her hands moved lightly along the spines as she read each title aloud.

No . . . No . . . No . . .

It was halfway through the final shelf that she saw the old pamphlet: *Beekeeping in the United States.*

She pulled it out slowly. It had been published in the 1930s by the U.S. Department of Agriculture and covered every aspect of beekeeping and honey processing. Didi had obtained it many years ago for an undergraduate biology course. She had written a paper on how bees dance to communicate the location of pollen sources.

She opened the pamphlet and smiled as she

read parts of the old-fashioned table of contents:

Nectar and pollen plants
Beekeeping regions in the United States
Managing colonies for high honey yield
Bee behavior
Beehive and honey handling equipment.

Then she noticed the chapter heading: Diseases and pests of adult honeybees.

And she knew she had something! She turned to that chapter. Her eyes roamed over the subheadings: *Nosema Disease. Acarine Disease. Septicemia. Bee Paralysis. Wax Moth.*

And finally the subheading *Bee Lice.*

She read with growing excitement.

"The bee louse is not a true parasite. It survives by tricking honeybees into disgorging by tapping them on the lips just as the hive workers do, while signaling for the transfer of a nectar load. The greatest damage is from the burrowing of the lice larvae in the cappings of the honeycomb."

Didi spun around happily and flung the little book onto her bed. She had broken the secret code of the poem. Bee lice. Massaging the lips of the honeybee. You get nectar or you get death. If you're a louse.

But wait a minute, she thought suddenly. So

she'd broken the code. So what? So Ida Day had been a beekeeper of sorts. And Burt Conyers had written a poem with a veiled reference to bees. So what?

The poem was as false a trail as you could follow. You're taking off for the stratosphere again, she cautioned herself. Isn't it about time you started acting like a scientist again instead of a conclusion-jumping idiot? The bee louse, *Braulu coeca* Nitzsch, is just what it is—no matter how many times it appears in a poem.

She folded her arms primly and tried to calmly think the matter through . . . to lay out what was known and sort it out from what was not yet known . . . to act like the scientist she was.

In a sense it was quite simple and clear: A reclusive old woman who earned her living as an herbalist and beekeeper was murdered during a robbery. The actual murder took place in the field adjoining her cottage.

The murderer, a young recovering drug addict, was caught, tried, and sent to prison thanks to the good police work of young Allie Voegler.

Seven years later a reclusive middle-aged man is murdered in the same field. He is the last of a very old Hillsbrook family. He was the driving force behind the now disbanded Hillsbrook Hunt Club and the current head of the local animal welfare league.

The police have a suspect in this second murder, but not enough evidence to charge him.

An outside investigator, Dr. Nightingale, then uncovers videotape evidence that the second killing, Breitland's, was a mistake. The intended target was an eccentric poet, Burt Conyers.

There is little to connect the two murder victims and the intended victim. Ida Day and Burt Conyers did once work in a Breitland-owned factory, which has been closed since the 1970s. And Conyers wrote a poem with an esoteric reference to bee lice, while Ida Day had been a beekeeper.

Didi realized her veterinary skills were not going to be of much help in the case. In vet work one goes from symptoms to the disease. A cow with stringy milk. A goat with loose stool and no appetite. A dog with runny eyes. A house cat with fever and lower back pain.

These abnormalities clue the vet, help her conduct an intelligent examination, enable her to make a correct diagnosis, lead her inexorably toward a solution, i.e., treatment.

But that was veterinary work. She was now faced with something that required a different kind of reasoning and detective work.

And she already knew what the disease was: murder.

In this case the symptoms were the problem. They seemed absurd—without logic.

What were the scattered symptoms?

Her friend Rose Vigdor tells people that the second murder to take place in Lubin's Field was inevitable because Ida Day was a witch and the field is haunted.

Someone gets worried about even a bizarre connection being made between the two killings and shoots Rose's dog as a warning to her to keep her mouth shut and mind her own business.

Meanwhile, Allie Voegler becomes violent when questioned about the Ida Day murder and the young man who went to prison for committing the crime.

John Breitland, victim number two, turns out not only to have been a recluse but a man who stripped his house of every memento of what he seems to have loved best—the Hillsbrook Hunt Club.

Someone places a bouquet of flowers on the supposed grave of Ida Day a short time after the Breitland murder. The flowers are wrapped in the newspaper account of Breitland's death.

A certain Mrs. Donniger reveals that the real reason John Breitland closed down the hunt club is some tragedy that befell several of its foxhounds.

And there were other snippets, perhaps equally meaningless—such as the fact that Ida

Day's biggest seller was some kind of herbal tea.

Didi leaned forward and buried her face in her hands.

Then, resolutely, she jumped up, walked down the stairs and into the kitchen, made herself a mug of sweet tea, cut herself a healthy wedge of sharp New York State cheddar cheese, and returned to her bedroom.

She drank the tea and ate the cheese in her mother's rocker, staring out the window across the fields and into the pine forest.

When she finished the repast, she just sat there gloomily. How quickly the bubble had burst. She had been flying high after the video revelation and the memory of the poem. Now she was back on the ground. No, stuck in the mud was more like it.

She simply had no idea what to do next. But she had to do something.

Why not question Burt Conyers? Did he know he had been the intended victim? Why would anyone want to shoot him? It made sense to ask him those questions. But Didi knew the man was so eccentric that anything he said was really blank verse and would have to be interpreted like his "nectar or death" couplet.

No, that wasn't the way to go.

She ran through her list of symptoms. Maybe

a search through all the florist records in the area to see who had obtained paper-whites. That way she could find out who put the bouquet on Ida Day's grave. But she realized that paper-white bulbs were available from all kind of sources other than florists. Even some convenience stores in Delaware County sold them out of barrels.

No, that was not the way to go either.

What about checking Mrs. Donniger's rather strange tale about the foxhounds? Just to get it out of the way—it probably meant nothing even if it was true. In fact, anything to do with Breitland might be meaningless now, since the intended victim was Conyers.

Didi stood up and went to the window. If Breitland's hounds had been hurt, he would have consulted a vet. Probably Mortimer Grissom. Ten years ago he was the most respected vet in Hillsbrook. Yes, it would be Doc Grissom.

But he had retired and now lived in a place called Titusville, on the east coast of Florida, near Cape Canaveral.

Didi walked to the phone, dialed local information, got the area code for Titusville, then called Information there for Grissom's number.

He answered on the first ring with a gruff "Grissom here!"

"Doc, it's Didi Nightingale . . . from Hillsbrook."

There was a long pause. Grissom seemed to be bringing together his aging synapses. He got them together. "How good to hear from you! I hear your practice is going real good."

"Well, I'm making a living," she said modestly. "But I want to ask you about something, Doc. Did you hear about the John Breitland murder?"

"Oh I did! Wasn't that something! Just terrible. Hillsbrook is getting like Miami."

"I need your help, Doc."

"Sure. What have you got?"

"I want to ask you about Breitland's foxhounds. A woman named Lilly Donniger—"

The old vet interrupted her excitedly. "It's amazing you should ask me that. I was thinking about his foxhounds the minute after I heard what had happened to him."

"Why so?"

"Well, the last time I saw him was under very strange circumstances. I was home in Hillsbrook. It was one in the morning. My wife had died only three months before. I couldn't sleep anymore. I was reading. The front bell rings. I opened the door and there's John. He says it's an emergency and asks me to follow him. We walk to his station wagon. The back gate was open. It was a terrible sight. Five foxhounds were lying in the back, side by side. Each one was covered by a bloody blanket. Each one was shot through the head. I asked him what happened. He said he had shot them to put them out of their pain and misery. 'From what?' I ask him. He wouldn't answer. All he said was that I must make sure they were all dead . . . that they were no longer suffering. I looked at the dogs. Of course they were dead. They had obviously been dead for hours. Rigor had already set in. No, he wanted me to examine each dog. So I searched for a pulse on each. Of course, there was none. He was satisfied. He thanked me, closed the door, and drove off. The damnest thing, isn't it?"

"Do you have any idea what happened to the dogs? I mean, before he shot them?"

"No idea," said Grissom. "It all happened so quickly. It was mighty strange."

Didi thanked him. He told her he would be up in Hillsbrook in a few months, on a visit. Didi said she hoped he would look her up. Of course he would, Doc Grissom replied. He'd love to see what the bright new vet was up to.

Didi sat back down slowly. A chill came over her. She closed her eyes and rocked. A terrible possibility was presenting itself in her mind . . . a warped, vicious, vengeful, murderous scenario.

As if Doc Grissom were a spider and his words had taken on life and were spinning their own web at great speed.

She opened her eyes wide as if to blot out the ugliness of the possibility. She stood up and walked to her chest, opened the top drawer, and removed a map.

She spread the map of Dutchess County out on the quilt. Her finger located Lubin's Field. Her thumb located the "coursing" route of the Hillsbrook Hunt.

She stepped back away from the bed. She picked up the shawl from behind the rocker, draped it over her shoulders, and once more walked downstairs and into the kitchen. On the way she looked into the mirror. "Lo, I have become a witch, like Ida Day," she said to herself, bringing the shawl even tighter around her neck.

Mrs. Tunney was busy near the stove.

"I'll be sleeping away from home tonight," Didi told her.

Mrs. Tunney nodded. There was a slight twitch of censure in the movement of her mouth, as if Didi had announced she was spending the night with a strange man.

"Tell Charlie to be sure to write down all the phone messages," Didi added.

"I will, Miss Quinn."

"Where is Trent Tucker?"

"In the barn."

Didi left by the kitchen door. Two of the yard

dogs started to frisk about her, trying to entice her to play. She ignored them and walked on.

The barn door was open. She could see Trent Tucker. He was splitting apples in two and feeding one half to Promise Me, throwing the other half in to Sara the sow's pen. Her piglets, now separated from their mother, were squealing at the indignity.

Tucker noticed the young doctor then. "The fall you took didn't bother your horse at all, Miss Quinn."

Didi walked over to him. "I want to borrow your rifle," she said.

He was astonished by the request and stood there looking at her, unable to answer.

"You heard me, didn't you?" Didi said.

"But I don't have a rifle anymore. You told us to get rid of them. Remember? Maybe Charlie's still got his old shotgun."

"Don't lie to me, Trent."

"I'm not! Believe me. I got rid of my deer rifle." He paused and looked at Promise Me, as if the horse could provide help. Then he added, "I still have my varmint rifle, of course. But it's an old twenty-two. I used to get woodchucks with it. But that ain't the kind of thing you meant—right?"

"Do you have any bullets?"

"Well . . . yeah."

"Go and get it."

"Now?"

"Yes. Right now."

Trent Tucker shrugged. Then he walked into the small tack room and shut the door behind him. Didi heard him digging in one of the trunks.

He came back with the rifle and a box of cartridges.

"Load it, will you," Didi said.

Tucker placed the bullets into the slide, one by one.

"Now tell me how I shoot it. If I have to."

He did a strange double take, but put up no argument. "You take the safety off," he instructed. "Here. And then you lever it once. The lever action brings the round into the chamber. So it's all ready to fire. Pull the trigger . . . here."

He handed the weapon over.

"What are you hunting, Doc?"

"Elephants and kangaroos," she said.

Trent Tucker shrugged.

"I'm going to need a blanket," Didi said.

The young man went back into the tack room and fetched one.

Didi wrapped the rifle in the faded plaid coverlet.

"You sure look like you're going on the warpath," Tucker said, almost chuckling.

"First I'm going to take a nap," she replied. She walked into the stall and lay down on the fresh hay. Promise Me ambled over and bumped her once with his nose. Then he lost interest.

Charlie Gravis handed an eight-dollar bouquet of flowers to Blanche at the door.

"I just thought you would like these," he said bashfully.

"They are *beautiful*. Absolutely *beautiful*. You always were a considerate man, Charles Gravis."

She opened the door wide and Charlie sauntered in. He felt a bit frisky.

Blanche put the flowers in a large cut glass vase and placed the vase on the floor, as if it were a statue.

After she'd admired the arrangement for a few moments she turned back to Charlie. "He's all ready," she said, and walked into the feline's room. Blanche returned with Yam in her arms.

Charlie blinked. The old yellow cat had obviously been brushed and coifed to a fare-the-well. And to top it off Blanche had loosely knotted a black silk ribbon around his neck.

Blanche took a seat, still hugging Yam tightly. The cat had a long-suffering and bored look on his face.

"Charlie," Blanche began, "I'm happy but a little . . . you know, frightened."

"What's there to be frightened about?" he replied quickly. For the first time he saw that there was a dot of black at the end of Yam's, or Wyatt Earp's, tail.

"What if they abuse him?" Blanche said worriedly. "What if poor Yam gets blinded by all those lights? What if he gets so frightened that he runs away?"

"There's nothing to worry about, Blanche. I'm telling you. I'll be watching him like a hawk."

"Oh, I know you will, Charlie. I know you will. It's just that . . ."

Her voice trailed off. She thrust Yam out away from her and turned him around so that she and the cat were face to face. "I know you're going to be a big star. I just know you're going to love every minute of it and they're all going to love you. There's nothing to be afraid of, baby."

Then she took Yam back onto her lap. "What are they going to call it, Charlie?"

"Call what?"

"The TV thing—the series."

"Well," he drawled, searching his mind for a reasonable lie, "I think the producer said something like *Days and Nights of a Country Vet*. It's only going to be about five episodes long."

Blanche let out a long, hard-to-define sigh, dropped the cat lightly onto the floor, went to the closet, and returned with an ancient dark metal cat carrier.

She opened the carrier top, stepped back, and seemed to hesitate, as if the thought of even a brief separation from precious Yam was too much to bear. She looked quickly at Charlie, the desperate question in her eyes: Is this worth it? He responded with an indulgent smile and an impassioned affirmative nod.

Blanche picked Yam up once more, deposited him in the box, and shut the lid. The cat did not struggle at all.

Charlie grabbed the carrier handle and after a few more reassurances that he would guard her treasure with his own life marched out of the house.

He hopped gamely into the pickup and placed the carrier on the seat between himself and Trent Tucker, who sat behind the wheel.

"What the hell is this?" young Tucker asked.

"What does it look like, you fool?"

Tucker leaned over and cracked the lid of the carrier. From inside, Yam glared murderously at him.

"Looks like a cat," he said. "A cat in a box."

"Send that boy to the head of the class," Charlie said.

"Old Tunney is *not* going to like this," Trent said. "She says there's no room for one single more animal at home. And that ain't nothing compared to what the good Doctor Quinn's going to say!"

Charlie was untroubled by the warning. "We ain't going home . . . yet," he said. "You're driving me over to Ike Badian's."

Although Trent Tucker had shown no curiosity about Charlie's maneuverings, a mile or so into the drive Charlie felt compelled to explicate the situation for his young companion.

He tapped the top of the cat carrier lightly. "This individual in here may look like a cat and walk like a cat. But he's much more than that. What we have here, Trent Tucker, is cash on the hoof. Or on the paw, I should say. This here is a moneymaking machine. This is our future, boy! Get me? Isn't it about time we start driving something other than this heap of tin? By God, it is. Know what I mean?"

Trent kept his eyes on the road during Charlie's speech. "Anything you say, Charlie," was the only response he made. His words had a cynical, patronizing cast that irritated Charlie to no end.

"Don't you understand what I'm trying to tell you, boy? This is Wyatt Earp we got here!"

Trent Tucker shot him an incredulous glance, as if the old man had lost his few remaining marbles and they were rolling all over the floor of the truck. But he was determined to say not a word. What would be the point? If this cat was

Wyatt Earp, then Trent was Doc Holiday. Everybody in the Nightingale house seemed to have a screw loose lately. Hadn't Miss Quinn hijacked his woodchuck rifle? He laughed to himself. What the hell—maybe this cat *was* Wyatt Earp, reincarnated. And, who knew, maybe *he* was Doc Holiday. What did that make Didi—Calamity Jane?

They reached the Badian farm. Trent Tucker parked by the side of the road. Charlie carried Yam up the driveway and past the house. He stopped when he saw Ike, who was sitting on the porch step smoking a cigar. Charlie gave him the World War II aviator's thumbs-up sigh. Ike grunted.

Charlie headed for the barn. There was still some light left in the day. The barn doors were still swung open on their tracks.

He put the carrier down just outside the doors and peered inside the barn. The cows were in their stalls. They looked nervous, swaying a bit; chewing their cuds with roving, shifty eyes.

He could hear the soft chattering of the invading hordes—the field mice and their allies.

Charlie looked down at the cat carrier. "All I want to say to you, Wyatt, is that I was the best friend your Al Hobson ever had. I know you've had a tough time of it these last few years. That Blanche just kept on insulting you—calling you sweet pussycat and all that lovey-dovey stuff. But now I'm giving you your chance. The chance to get your reputation back ... to be a man again. And when this is all over I'm going to give you something real to eat. Understand? None of that fool canned food. I mean raw liver and heavy cream and sardines with the skin still on 'em."

He went down on arthritic knees and opened the carrier lid. "Okay, Wyatt Earp. You go clean out Tombstone. Do it for me, and for Ike. Let's go, boy!"

The yellow cat hopped out and looked around. Then he slowly and solemnly walked inside.

Charlie Gravis closed the barn doors behind him.

"What's this—a house call?" Rose Vigdor asked.

"Kind of," Didi said. She walked over to the wounded dog, who was now doing quite well. Aretha had just finished a bowl of chicken soup. Her canine companions milled around her, unhappy. They had been given no soup.

"She's much, much better," Rose said. Didi looked the dog over without touching her. Aretha liked the attention. She cocked her head and whined a little.

"Okay, Rose," Didi said resolutely once she

was satisfied with Aretha's progress, "down to business. I need your help."

"Of course, of course!" There had been something in Didi's voice—an urgency—that made Rose react with passion. Then she noticed the object that Didi had brought with her. "What is that?"

Didi unrolled the old blanket.

"Why are you carrying a rifle around with you?" Rafael asked, suddenly afraid.

Didi held up her hands, indicating she would explain shortly. "Can we sit down for a minute?"

Rose led her into that section of the unfinished barn renovation that functioned as the living room. It had three makeshift chairs. The two women sat.

"Can you get me a pad and pencil?" Didi requested.

The items were delivered into her hands. Didi looked at the point for a moment, stared up at the scaffolding, then put pencil to paper. She wrote steadily, for about five minutes. Rose waited, confused, fidgeting.

Then Didi ripped the two sheets from the pad and handed them to her friend.

"I'm not much of a scriptwriter," she said, "but please read this out loud."

Rose fiddled with the papers. "Out loud?"

"Yes. In your normal speaking voice."

"But I don't *have* a normal speaking voice," she quipped. She noticed then that Didi wasn't smiling, so she just began to read in as flat a voice as she could manage:

"My name is Mona Farr. I'm calling from the Owl Motel just outside Hillsbrook, but my home is Vermont. I'm here for one reason only. To get justice in the distribution of John Breitland's estate. I went to the lawyer handling the case. He threw me out of his office. He wouldn't even look at the literally hundreds of intimate letters I brought with me. Letters John Breitland wrote to me over the past fifteen years, during which time I was his loving and faithful common law wife. I am begging for help from anyone in Hillsbrook. I and my two children, both fathered by John Breitland, deserve justice."

Rose looked up.

"Well done," said Didi.

"Thank you. What is this crap?"

"I told you: a script. In about an hour, if you are willing to help me, I want you to call a radio station from the Owl Motel and read it."

"Why?"

"Because I believe the killer out there will go to any lengths to obtain those nonexistent intimate letters sent from John Breitland to his common law wife."

"The killer of who? Ida Day? John Breitland?"

"There have been more murders than the ones you mentioned, Rose. Murders most horrible."

"Who?"

"It's too ugly to talk about now. And too complicated. Will you help me out, Rose?"

"Why don't you make the call yourself?"

"Because I met this radio talk show host and he might recognize my voice. His name's Jim Bartolo. The show is on WKDF at around seven this evening."

"Is this Bartolo the killer?"

"No, of course not. He's not involved at all."

"I used to listen to his program sometimes," Rose mused, "until my radio batteries ran out."

"We don't have much time," Didi said.

Rose looked nervously at the rifle. "Look, Night Gown, you know I want to help. You know I'd do anything for you. But you frighten me with this. This weapon frightens me. It's all so—"

"Listen, Rose! Imagine someone dropped a coin on a nice lawn. At the end of a year's time after the coin was dropped it would no longer be visible. It would be about an inch beneath the surface. In thirty years it'll be thirty inches below. Earthworms, Rose. The earthworms turn the soil over and the coin is buried deeper. That's what we're facing now. Time! The accelerated vanishing of all evidence. The way I see it, what I propose is a shot in the dark. But it's our only shot. It makes sense."

"My dogs, Didi. What will I do with my dogs?"

"Can't you leave them alone for a few hours?"

Rose began to pace. "I suppose I could."

"You don't have to bring anything with you except that piece of paper. Neither of us has Vermont plates, so I'll park the jeep a hundred yards or so away and we'll just walk in and register. They don't ask any questions at the Owl Motel. It's a dive."

At 6:45 P.M. Mona Farr and her sister Lucia checked into the Owl Motel, three miles outside of Hillsbrook on an old truck route. The room clerk, a young man with earphones on, didn't even look at them as he slid the key over to Mona.

Their room was a small box with two windows and bright red, dirt-streaked curtains. The sagging bed took up most of the space.

There was a television that didn't work, a working radio and cassette player, and a working telephone.

Didi and Rose sat silently on the bed, side by side. Didi had laid her wristwatch on the small table next to the phone.

The radio was on the only other piece of furniture in the room: a small writing desk. At seven o'clock Didi got off the bed and switched on the radio, tuning it to WKDF. Jim Bartolo greeted his listeners and gave out the number to call. Then he started his nightly roundup of events.

"Okay, Rose. Make the call now," she said.

Rose took a deep breath, picked up the receiver, and dialed.

She put her hand over the mouthpiece. "It's a recording. It says to hold on; the phone will keep ringing until he's ready to take your call. We'll be on seven-second delay. When he picks up we should turn down the radio."

Didi nodded. The first call Bartolo took was from a woman complaining about the town dump. The second caller, who sounded like a very old man, talked incoherently about national politics. Bartolo dispensed with the two of them quickly.

"I'm on!" Rose hissed, taking her hand from the microphone. Didi hurried to lower the volume of the radio. Rose had already launched into her reading of the script. When the speech was finished Didi returned the volume to normal.

Bartolo was laughing. "Look, lady," he said derisively, "if you are who you claim to be, you should call the Hillsbrook Police Department. But you may just be one of the buzzards circling a couple of hundred thousand choice acres up for grabs."

Then he went to a station break. Didi snapped off the radio. "You were great, Rose."

"What do we do now?"

"We wait. Just wait. Let's straddle the door on either side."

"Won't that be dangerous? This crazy person will probably smash down the door to get to those letters."

"I doubt it. Ten bucks to the desk clerk will get our key. All the clerk needs is an excuse—like, we're waiting for our visitor and he wants to surprise us, or he doesn't want to wake us. He'll have thought of something credible to tell the desk guy. He'll know the name you used to check in."

"How will he—" Rose stopped there. "Are we sure it's a 'he'?"

"No."

"Well, how will he or she know my name?"

"Because you just gave it out over the air, Rose."

"Oh. That's right. I did, didn't I?"

They settled in, one on each side of the door, their backs against the wall and their legs stretched out. The rifle, still in its blanket, lay across Didi's knees.

At nine o'clock Didi walked over to the other

side of the room and flicked the wall switch off. The room went dark.

Rose began one of her funny, ribald, often self-deprecating monologues. This one was the story of the way her two male dogs had reacted when she brought Aretha home after her recuperative stay in Didi's clinic.

The story seemed to go on and on. Didi wasn't listening to the words anymore; she was listening to Rose's growing discomfort, which threatened at any moment to turn into panic. What right do I have, Didi thought, to subject Rose to his? To keep her here all night. She helped me out. She's done her job. Isn't the rest of it my responsibility? Didn't I hatch this whole plot?

"Why don't you take the jeep back home now?" she said suddenly to Rose. "Really, I can handle this myself."

"It's too late for that, Didi. I'm hooked. The killer is going to sneak in at two in the morning or something, with a flashlight and a knife that long; and he's going to creep up to the bed to press the knife against Mona Farr's pretty throat and demand those letters. Now, why would I want to split and miss something like that? What am I, crazy?"

So Rose remained. By ten o'clock she was fast asleep.

At midnight Didi dozed off, too.

At one that morning a man with a flashlight
and a knife did indeed open the door of their
room and slip in.

Rose woke when she saw the beam of light
shining on the bed. "Didi, is that you?" she
called.

Didi opened her eyes. She saw the shadow.
"The light, Rose!" she screamed. "Hit the light
switch!"

The shadow dropped the flashlight and ran
for the door.

Didi blocked his access. The shadow grabbed
her by the arm and flung her aside easily, slamming her head against the wall in the process.
She rolled the rifle out of the blanket, her hands
fumbling for the safety.

But too late. The man was out of the door and
running.

Didi stepped into the doorway. "Stop!" she
screeched at the top of her lungs. But Shadow
did not stop. She levered a round in the chamber and fired. Shadow stumbled. She fired
again. This time, he fell.

She ran out. He was writhing on the ground.

"Who is it? Who is it?" Rose, behind her, was
shouting desperately.

The man rolled over onto his back, his right
arm outstretched.

It was Jed Benteen, director of the Sun House
drug rehab center.

* * *

Mrs. Tunney began serving the oatmeal. Charlie heaped cream and brown sugar on his portion. This caught Mrs. Tunney's eye.

"Since when do you doctor your oatmeal like that? You're not a spring chicken, Charlie. You should be ashamed of yourself. And you'll be dead if you keep doing it."

Charlie reflected for a moment. Was this the time to reveal that they were now in the presence of the Pied Piper of Dutchess County? At a thousand dollars a pop.

No. This was not the time. He would wait until he got the money. Maybe at lunchtime. He would just lay the bills out like slices of bologna on the table.

"I just feel good. It's a beautiful morning," was all he said.

Trent Tucker was buttering his toast with broad slashes of the butter knife. "I heard over the radio there was a shooting over at the Owl Motel last night."

"Who shot who?" Charlie inquired.

"They didn't say."

"Hey, where were you last night?" Charlie asked mischievously.

"That's not funny!" Mrs. Tunney interjected.

"But we all know our little Trent Tucker used to take his girlfriends to the Owl, Mrs. T. The ones he'd pick up at that bar. What's the name of that place—Jim's?"

"Jack's," Trent Tucker corrected. "Like you don't know, Charlie. And I was only in the Owl Motel twice in my life. The last time being a year ago."

"That's the last time you had more than ten cents in your pocket."

Abigail found Charlie's comment very funny. She laughed her low, mellifluous laugh, which seemed to end the conversation.

When they finished their oatmeal, they all waited for Mrs. Tunney to make her usual egg offer. But she was oddly silent.

Trent Tucker lifted one edge of his bowl and let it drop to the table loudly, trying to break the old lady's reverie. It worked. Mrs. Tunney looked up at them.

But she didn't offer to make eggs. "I'm worried about Miss Quinn," she said.

"Why? Because she stayed out all night?" Charlie asked.

"Yes. And she's not back yet."

"She's a big girl now, Mrs. Tunney."

"Oh, I know that. But I hope she's not in bed with that big fool of a policeman."

Charlie grimaced. "Amen to that!"

Abigail sat back, smiled, and recited:

> Love is not love
> Which alters when it

alteration finds,
Or bends with the remover
to remove,
Oh no! It is an ever-fixed
mark.

One and all, they ignored her. "I tried so hard over the past few years," Mrs. Tunney complained, "to get her a nice man. But it just didn't work out."

"Nope, it never did," Charlie echoed.

"And I'm going to keep trying. Her mother would be turning over in her grave if she knew where Missy was."

Charlie nodded. "It's a bad match. That's for sure, Mrs. T."

"That Voegler has nothing going for him but a job. And Miss Quinn is so pretty and smart."

Charlie repeated his "Amen."

"Eggs?" Trent Tucker called loudly. He muttered under his breath, "Jeez! It's only one night. What have you two old coots got against a person getting it once in a while?"

Abigail held her bowl out, too, and broke into a wide grin.

Allie sat up abruptly. His clock read 6:20 A.M. Who the hell was ringing his doorbell at this hour?"

He walked to the window and peered down.

It was Wynton Chung in uniform. Allie buzzed him in and waited at the door.

"What's up?" he asked Chung with worry in his voice. The young officer looked a little shaken.

"There was trouble at the Owl Motel last night," Chung said.

Allie shrugged. Trouble at the Owl. That was no reason to wake him.

"A shooting," Chung said. "Your friend was involved."

"My friend? What friend?"

"The lady vet."

Allie stepped back as if he had been shoved, hard. The pulse at the side of his neck began to pound. He took a deep breath before speaking. "Is she okay?" His voice could have been that of a child.

"She wasn't shot, Allie. She was the shooter."

"Are you crazy, man? What are you saying— Didi shot somebody? You must be high or something."

Chung brushed aside Allie's insults and took him by the arm. "Come on. She's at Samaritan Hospital. Put some clothes on. I'll take you over there."

Allie listened as Chung talked on the ride to the hospital.

"She and her friend Rose Vigdor checked into the Owl at around six-fifteen last night. They registered under the names Mona and Lucia Farr. Sisters. One of them called the Bartolo radio show a little after seven and claimed to have letters from John Breitland proving she's his common law wife and entitled to his estate. At one in the morning Jed Benteen got a key from the clerk—"

"Who got a key?"

"Jed Benteen. The guy who runs Sun House. You know him."

"Yeah, I know him," Allie affirmed. "Keep talking."

"Benteen lets himself into their room after buying a key from the clerk and assuring him it's all a joke. He's carrying a flashlight and a knife. Some kind of altercation ensues. Benteen runs and Dr. Nightingale puts two bullets in him."

"He's not . . ."

"No, no. He's okay. One bullet in the forearm. One in the shoulder."

"What kind of weapon?"

"She used a twenty-two-caliber rifle."

"Benteen make a statement?"

"Yeah. He claims he was visiting a prostitute and entered the wrong room. Everybody panicked, he says."

"And Didi? What does she say?"

"Nothing."

"What do you mean, nothing?"

"She said she won't say a word until she sees you."

"What about Rose?"

"Same."

"Where is Rose now?"

"Back at her place. We cautioned her to stay put. Both women were treated for shock. Didi—I mean, your friend opted to wait in the hospital for you."

"Is there a guard on Benteen?"

"Sure. Hospital Security."

Allie didn't say any more until he walked into Samaritan Hospital and found Didi sitting on an emergency room bench. Her face was drained. Her hands were clasped on her lap as if she had been a bad girl who'd been ordered to sit in the corner.

"So," Allie began, "I hear you got a hunting license."

She didn't answer. She touched the bench, indicating that he should sit down beside her.

"For a lady who always gave me such a hard time about hunting, you sure did a fast turn-around. But at least you don't go after deer, like me. Too easy for you, Didi? Guess you like to go after the real big game."

He sat down then. And his voice cracked. "What a holy mess you got everybody in," he said. "But thank God you're okay."

"Are you finished?" she asked wearily.

"I haven't even started, Dr. Nightingale. Don't you understand you shot a man?"

"You got it wrong, Allie. I shot a rabid dog." It was a venomous statement and it startled Allie. The good doctor never talked of people in those terms.

"Listen to me, Allie. I have a terrible tale to tell."

He held his tongue and listened.

"Ida Day and Burt Conyers became friends when they worked together at the Breitland factory a long time ago.

"Their friendship was based on a consuming hatred of the Breitland family. I don't know why—I don't know what the Breitlands ever did to them—but the hatred was there and it festered and went on festering long after the plant closed.

"Then, they acted on their hatred. One day they moved Ida's beehives into Lubin's Field. And they put dog bait down. On the hives. The foxhounds were being run close by. Five of the hounds left the pack to get the bait. The bees went crazy. They attacked. The hounds were severely wounded. John Breitland shot all five to put them out of their misery.

"Breitland never recovered from the tragedy. He disbanded the Hillsbrook Hunt. He became a social recluse except for offering his services and money to an organization that alleviates the suffering of animals.

"And he harbored a desire for vengeance. He knew who did that to his foxhounds.

"The time came to extract that vengeance. Many people in Hillsbrook owed Breitland favors. One of them was Jed Benteen.

"Why? I don't really know. I didn't even know it was Benteen until he broke into our room last night. But it all makes sense. All the drug rehab centers had terrible trouble with the banks and zoning laws. Benteen must have asked Breitland for help. And Breitland was now collecting. Maybe he had lent Benteen money and would forgive the debt for this favor.

"Anyway, Benteen and an associate murdered Ida Day in Lubin's Field, right where Breitland's dogs were stung into oblivion. Mosely, that young man who went to prison for the murder, was framed. The wrong man was sent to prison, and ultimately to his death. I am sorry, Allie, really sorry, but that is the truth. You arrested the wrong man.

"Breitland wasn't finished yet, though. He waited. He brooded. And then came the lucky break for him. The Blessing of the Animals.

"John Breitland learned that the blessing would take place in Lubin's Field. And Burt Conyers would be reciting. He reactivated the murder team. The target was the poet. The gunman was in place. He aimed. He fired. But, at the last moment, a dog fight caused Conyers to turn aside. The bullet killed Breitland instead.

"Then Benteen heard over the radio a woman who claims to be Breitland's common law wife. And she's claiming to have hundreds of intimate letters from him. Did Breitland reveal anything to this woman about the Ida Day murder in those letters? Or the connection—either legal or financial—between Breitland and Sun House? Benteen realized he had to obtain those letters.

"And he tried to. Last night. Except it turned out there were no letters, and no wife either. There's only two frightened women in a cheap motel room."

"And one rifle," Allie added.

"Yes. One rifle."

There followed a long silence. Allie kept his eyes straight ahead. Then he got up slowly, walked to the water fountain, took a drink, and sat back down.

"It sounds like a *Star Wars* fantasy, Didi. Did you ever think of writing fiction for a living?"

She turned swiftly and put her hand on his arm. "It's the truth, Allie."

"The truth? Well, maybe. But in my line of work I need something called evidence."

"You've surely got enough corpses."

"Yeah, but they're all buried."

"And there's a lot more."

"Like what!"

"We know Ida and Conyers both worked at the factory. We know Breitland was deranged from the terrible thing that happened to his dogs. I spoke to the vet he consulted that night. We know Rose's dog was shot as a warning to her after she went around shooting her mouth off about the murders in Lubin's Field. We know that the foxhounds were regularly run right alongside Lubin's Field. We know, at least I'm pretty sure, that Burt Conyers placed a bouquet on Ida's grave after Breitland was killed—a sentimental gesture because he knew who had killed her, and why. We know that Benteen came to the hotel last night to steal those letters."

Voegler exploded in anger then. "We know . . . we know . . . we know. You keep repeating that goddamn phrase over and over. Who is this 'we'? Are you pregnant? It sure doesn't include me. I don't know nothing."

She did not respond.

"Sorry for yelling," he said when he had calmed down a bit. "Let's try and be rational. Both of us. First things first. You shot a man, Didi. You and I both know that no grand jury would indict you considering the fact that Benteen entered your room illegally and with a knife. You're going to be in the clear, but believe me, they'll make you go through hoops before they turn you loose."

"I fully understand that."

"Good. I have work to do. I've got to go now. Is there anything you want me to do?"

"When are you going to charge Benteen?"

"With breaking and entering, you mean? He claims he stumbled into your room by mistake. He claims the clerk gave him the wrong key. He claims he was there to visit a hooker."

"You don't believe that, do you?"

"I don't know what to believe, Didi. I don't even know if I believe a bee sting can kill a fox-hound."

"You weren't listening to me, Allie. The hounds were severely wounded by those bee stings. It was John Breitland who shot them—to put them out of their pain. But as a matter of fact, they would have died from the stings. Multiple bites like that will kill a dog, any kind of dog. Bee venom is like snake venom. It attacks the heart and the circulation. That's why bee-keepers wear protective netting. A bee bite is *not* a mosquito bite. And a hundred bees stinging you right now, Allie, could easily kill *you*."

"I'll pick up some netting when I get a chance," he said wryly.

He started for the emergency room exit, but then turned back to her. "Tell me the truth, Didi. Why did you shoot him?"

"I was frightened. He ran, he wouldn't stop. I . . . shot . . . I mean, I don't know why, Allie. In my opinion the man is at least a double murderer. But I don't feel good about what happened. I feel miserable, as a matter of fact."

He walked out without further comment. Outside, Chung was leaning against the side of the patrol car. Allie turned and stared at himself in the reflecting glass door of the hospital entrance. He wondered how he would look in one of those protective netting getups that the beekeepers wore, those things that looked like an elaborate lady's hat with a veil.

It was absurd, in light of everything that was going on, to be thinking of something like that. Yet that is what he was doing. He was so distracted by the image that he didn't hear Chung calling to him.

Yeah, right, Allie was thinking. The protective netting would have to be of a very fine mesh to keep the deadly bees away from your face—less like a lady's hat and more like the fine mail face guards of the medieval knights.

What was this? Was his memory pulling him back to his childhood, when he played with the pieces of his pop's plastic chess set? No.

No, it wasn't that at all. The memories were much more recent that that. He had seen that netting somewhere recently, very recently.

"Hey, Allie! Are you deaf?" Wynton Chung was standing beside him now.

"Huh?" Allie forced himself back into the moment.

"I said, should I run you home?"

"No. Drop me in town. By the health food store."

Chung laughed. "You look like you could use a shot of something healthy. What's the matter with you?"

Allie shrugged the question off.

"Wait for me," he said when they reached the store. Allie peered into the shop window. The store wasn't open yet but Harland Frick was inside reading a newspaper and drinking coffee.

"I need to talk to you, Harland," he said, stepping across the threshold and almost shoving the merchant out of the way.

"It's a little early in the day, isn't it?" Frick said weakly.

Allie ignored the comment. "I need to talk to you," he repeated, "about Sonny James and that girlfriend of his. Paula's her name." The unspoken assumption was that Harland, being the town busybody, was the person to consult for such information.

"I don't know much of anything about them. Only that they live on the Ridge."

"What I want to know is simple: Have they known each other long?"

"Oh yes. A very long time. They were, shall we say, childhood sweethearts." Frick allowed himself a chuckle. "That's a rather old-fashioned expression, isn't it? Especially applied to—well, Sonny isn't the most sentimental fellow I've ever met. Anyway, people don't say that much anymore, do they—'childhood sweethearts'?"

"No, I guess they don't."

"Actually I thought you were going to ask me about the shooting last night. When I saw you at the window that's what I thought. Who would believe it? Rose Vigdor and Didi Nightingale. Imagine those two holing up at a cheap motel and then shooting a man! It's just—"

"Thanks a lot, Harland," Allie said, cutting him off. "I'll let you get back to your breakfast."

"Well, just a minute, Allie. Wouldn't you think that if anybody would do a thing like that—acting like Bonnie and Clyde—it would be Sonny James and Paula? I mean, Rose comes from the city. But I would hardly expect this from Didi. After all, she *is* a doctor."

"Yep," Allie said as he left, "you're right about that, Harland." He waved good-bye and hurried to join Chung in the patrol car.

"I'm going to need you for a short while more," he told Chung.

"Sure."

"Drive me to Sonny James's place on the Ridge."

Once on the premises, Allie didn't hesitate. He walked right into the large tent.

"Look who's here!" Sonny called out in false cheerfulness. "The only moose ever seen in Dutchess County."

Paula was silent. She looked down at the torn shirt in her lap. There was a spool of thread and a needle nearby.

Allie walked over to her. "Sorry to break up your sewing circle, Paula. But we're going for a little drive. Let's go."

"Where to?" she said sullenly.

"Just around."

She looked to Sonny for help.

"Do what the man says," he advised calmly. "He's got the badge and the gun." Then he laughed nastily. "And he's got the antlers."

Paula followed Allie out of the tent and into the back seat of the cruiser. Chung, at the wheel, did not speak.

Allie gave driving instructions. Chung took off.

"Where are you taking me, man?" Paula demanded.

"For a drive in the country. Like I said, Paula. A drive down memory lane."

Close to her, he found Paula even more sexually attractive. There was a kind of nervousness about her; a kind of intense nervousness that he was responding to. He wondered for a moment how he could find both Paula and Didi Nightingale sexy. They were so different in looks, temperament, style.

The car shot past the town dump. "You've taken this ride before, Paula?" Allie asked innocuously.

"Everybody in Hillsbrook drives to the dump," she answered, sitting erect on the car seat, her hands on the top of her knees, her fingers drumming some kind of imaginary song.

Allie called out more instructions to Wynton Chung.

"We're going to English Springs, Paula. You've been there, haven't you?"

"What the hell do you want with me?"

"Why so unfriendly, Paula? I thought you and me would get along just fine. Don't you like big old country cops? You and me are the salt of the earth, aren't we?"

She smirked but remained silent.

"Officer Chung," Allie addressed his colleague, "Paula's friend called me a moose. Should I take that as a compliment or an insult? Enlighten me, would you?"

Chung made eye contact with Allie in the mirror above his head, but he did not answer. He increased the speed of the vehicle. Allie could feel the sweat accumulating at his armpits. From now on, he realized, he had to make every word and gesture count.

Nothing more was said until they reached the dump at English Springs.

"Wait here," Allie ordered Chung. "You, get out!" he told Paula.

He led her to the edge of the pit. She stopped short at the truck ramp.

"Walk down," he said.

"I'm not going down there."

"Walk or get carried. Those are the two choices."

She looked around as if seeking help from an invisible someone. There was no help forthcoming. She descended slowly, Allie close behind her.

"Now turn left," he said, "and go about fifty feet. To where you dumped those bags the other night."

Paula gave him a startled look.

He smiled. "Didn't you know you and Sonny have been under surveillance since the Breitland murder? I can't believe a smart lady like you wouldn't have figured that out. I was right behind you, Paula." He pulled out a pad from his back pocket and waved it in front of her like a trophy. "It's all in here, in my report book. Oh, how juries love these little suckers. There's just something so . . . authentic . . . about a cop's little black notebook."

Paula walked to the spot where she had dumped the black plastic bags. Allie bent and began to dig around in the junk. In a few minutes he had the small lamp he had looked at a few days ago.

"Why would you dump something like this, Paula? Isn't this lovely? Sure, the wiring is a bit frayed. But still . . . well, I wouldn't have thrown it away."

She stared at the lamp, saying nothing.

"Notice the shade, Paula. It's real unusual, isn't it? Have you ever seen anything like it before? Looks like it's made out of mesh—some kind of netting. Do know what it was originally?"

When she refused to talk, he went on. "It was originally part of a beekeeper's protective face covering. This one covered Ida Day's face. But in time it got torn a bit, so she made a lampshade out of it. Nice, huh? Now let me tell you the strange part. The part that explains how the lamp ended up here in this dump.

"See, years ago your true love Sonny killed an old woman. He looted her cottage and gave the objects in it to Jed Benteen. Benteen stashed them in the room of a kid at Sun House. The kid's name was Lou Mosely. But Sonny's got a weakness for junk, as you know. Old stuff—radios, old coffeepots, anything. This lamp must have caught his fancy, so he kept it. Until a few nights ago, that is. Until he did his spring cleaning. He probably forgot all about where this lamp came from. It was just another piece of junk and it was time to get rid of it."

Allie thrust the lamp at her. But Paula would not take it.

"Time to talk to me, Paula."

"I got nothing to say to you."

"No? That's too bad, Paula. Because right now a state trooper is arresting Sonny and another one is picking up Jed Benteen. They're both being charged with the murders of Ida Day and John Breitland."

That was a lie, of course. But Paula didn't know that. She had become unsteady on her feet and she was nervously pulling at her short hair.

"If you don't talk to me now, you're going to be facing accessory to murder charges. Something like that can send you away forever. If you talk to me now you'll end up doing very little time."

The young woman turned away and stared up at the rim of the dump. She mumbled something.

"I can't hear you!" Allie shouted.

Paula turned on him in a fury. "I said I'll talk to you!"

Trent Tucker was driving like a drunk.

"Keep your eyes on the damn road!" Charlie yelled.

"Yeah, yeah, okay. Man! I just can't believe Miss Quinn shot that guy with my rifle."

"Why did you give it to her?"

"What was I supposed to do—say no?"

"Well, at least the latest radio report says Benteen is doing good. There must be a whole lot we don't know. I mean, they didn't arrest Dr. Quinn."

"Why'd she do it, Charlie? What made her shoot that guy?"

"Shut up and drive, Trent Tucker." Charlie had more important things on his mind than his boss taking some target practice.

They reached the Badian farm a few minutes later. "You wait here for me," Charlie said. But he didn't move to get out of the truck. He sat there smiling at the mystery of it all. Here he was, old and broke, seated in a decrepit pickup truck.

Ah, but a few minutes from now . . . a few minutes from now things would be different; he would be utterly transformed. He'd have a thousand bucks in his pocket. He'd be the affluent, respected, sought-after Pied Piper of Dutchess County. And, if Miss Quinn had to hire a fancy lawyer, she'd be able to depend on old Charlie Gravis.

He sauntered out of the truck and made his way toward the barn.

The herd had already been turned out to pasture. Ike was standing by the pasture fence, chewing an unlit cigar and looking over the cows.

"Well, Ike?" Charlie boomed out as he approached him.

"Unbelievable!" Badian cried out, removing the cigar stub and grinning broadly.

"Didn't I tell you," Charlie crowed. "What did I tell you!"

"Just unbelievable," Ike repeated.

"Let me get Wyatt Earp and then I'll pick up the cash." He trotted over to the barn and bent down to pick up the empty cat carrier. Charlie entered the barn and walked down the quiet aisle.

"Where are you, Wyatt? Time to go home, buddy."

Yam—Wyatt Earp—was nowhere in sight.

Then Charlie heard a rustling sound from one of the stalls. He walked over and looked in.

"Oh my God!" The carrier fell from his hand with a clatter.

Charlie heard himself saying exactly the words Ike Badian had used: "Unbelievable!"

Wyatt Earp was on his back, snoozing happily. His whiskers were drenched with raw, rich, sweet milk.

All along the edge of the stall were field mice. There seemed to be hundreds and hundreds of them. Chattering, running, frolicking, their tufted little ears not even tilting toward their new friend.

Maybe, thought Charlie, I can become a cat-**sitter**.

It was three o'clock in the afternoon. Didi had come home from the hospital three hours ago. She had tried to sleep but the attempt had been futile.

Now she sat and rocked in the chair. A delayed reaction had set in. Tears and shame, one coming swiftly on the heels of the other, alternating.

The problem, she knew, was the bullet wounds in Benteen. She had actually pointed a weapon at another person and shot him. *Shot* him. It was the first time in her life she had ever hurt another human being.

No matter how many times she reconstructed the events, she really didn't know why she had fired on Benteen. Of course, if she hadn't fired . . . if he hadn't fallen . . . she never would have known the identity of the intruder. There was a chance the motel clerk could have identified him, but only a slight chance.

What astonished her and pained her even more was how expertly she had handled the rifle. As if she had been born to it.

Suddenly there was a knock at the door. She

grimaced. She had left orders that she was not to be disturbed.

Didi tried to ignore the rapping. But the knocker was persistent. "Yes?" she finally responded.

Mrs. Tunney did not exactly enter the room. Instead, she stuck her head in through the cracked door. "You have a visitor, Miss."

"Who?"

The housekeeper made a face. "That policeman. That Voegler man."

"All right. Send him up."

Allie came in and shut the door quietly behind him. He was carrying a long, slender package. "You've been crying," he said.

"True."

He handed the box to her. Didi undid the simple ribbon and opened the lid. "Oh, Allie. Yellow roses. They're beautiful. But what are they for?"

"Apology and appreciation."

"How poetic of you, Mr. Voegler."

"Not poetry. Fact. I'm apologizing for my behavior at the hospital today. And I'm appreciating how right you were— about everything."

"What led you to believe I was right about Benteen?"

Allie walked to the window and stared out. Then he looked back at her over his shoulder. "It's a pretty strange story, Didi."

"That's okay. I have nowhere to go."

"We've been watching Sonny James and his girl since the Breitland murder. A few nights ago she took some bags to the English Springs dump. I went through the stuff after she'd gone. There was a small lamp with a shade made out of mesh. I forgot about it. It meant nothing to me. Then, in the hospital you started talking about the bee stings and the protective mesh for beekeepers. When I left you I suddenly remembered the lamp. It had to have belonged to Ida Day. It had to be one of the things the murderer took from her cottage."

His voice broke then. He said in a pleading voice, "Believe me, Didi, I thought that kid Mosely was her killer. We found the loot in his room at Sun House. Now I know the kid was innocent. Now that it's too late!"

Didi looked down at the roses, still in her lap. She could not assuage his grief.

He steadied himself and continued. "Once I realized it was Ida's lamp, I knew that Sonny James's girlfriend was the weak link. *If* she knew Sonny at the time of the Day killing. I went to Harland Frick 'cause he knows just about everything about people in this town. He said Sonny and Paula were childhood sweethearts. So I took Paula to the dump and turned the pressure on her. She didn't require much pressuring. She confirmed almost everything you told me and cleared up a lot of the fuzzy details, too."

"Like what?" Didi asked.

"For one, why Ida and the poet Conyers hated the Breitlands so much—enough to ambush their foxhounds. It seems that Ida was old man Breitland's mistress for many years. When he died he didn't leave the woman a penny. As for Conyers's motive, he hated them because they threw half the town out of work when they closed the factory

"For another, why Benteen was so indebted to Breitland that he would commit murder for him—or at least hire Sonny James to do it. Sun House was built on land purchased from Breitland. Breitland sold him the land cheap, but then he financed the building and the whole operation. Breitland never demanded payment on that loan and Benteen was stupid enough to fall far behind. One day, Breitland called in his marker."

Allie walked away from the window. He stood near the rocking chair looking down at Didi. "You made only one mistake," he said.

"What was that?"

"You said the wrong man was killed, that it was an accident. It wasn't that way. Breitland ordered Benteen to kill Conyers that day in Lubin's Field, just as you said. But Benteen wanted to be free of Breitland. And he wanted

to make sure that Breitland could never impli-
cate him in the Ida Day murder and the subsequent frame-up. So he simply ordered Sonny to
ignore the poet and aim for Breitland. The aim
was true—dog fight or no."

He reached down and picked up the flowers
and he laughed. "Flowers and bees. It was the
bees that broke the case."

"How right you are," Didi agreed, thinking
again of the bee couplet in Burt's poem.

"Let me put these in water for you," Allie
said.

"There's no vase in this room."

"What should I do then?"

Slowly, Didi declaimed what she could remember of the bee couplet: "Touch my lips and
you will get nectar or death." She had no idea
why the words had come to her at just that moment.

Allie flung the box of flowers onto the bed. In
a single, fluid movement he lifted her from the
rocker and kissed her mouth.

She returned the kiss with equal passion. His
hands were all over her, kneading, stroking.

Didi pushed him away suddenly. "Not here,
Allie! Not now!"

"Why not?" he choked out.

"This was my mother's room."

"So what?"

She turned the question over in her mind

briefly. Then she echoed his words: "So what indeed." And she laughed and kissed him again.

"Oh," Blanche gushed as she pulled Yam out of his carrier and crushed him against her face, "he looks so happy. He looks like he enjoyed every minute."

"He sure did," Charlie replied glumly.

"Did he have a big scene?"

"Sure did. About five minutes' worth with the camera just on him doing his stuff," Charlie lied.

"You *are* going to be a star!" Blanche assured Yam, shaking him happily. Then she let him down. Yam ambled into the kitchen to inspect the dish Blanche had laid out for the star's homecoming.

"Are you in a big hurry, Charlie?" she asked excitedly.

"I have to be going shortly."

"Well, this won't take long. You just sit where you are." With that, she disappeared into the rear of the house.

Charlie stood in the doorway to the kitchen. The yellow cat turned his head and he and Charlie eyeballed each other. "One day I'll get even," Charlie swore.

When Blanche returned she was holding something up for his inspection. "Just take a look at this!" she demanded.

Charlie couldn't make out what it was.

"Don't you see?" She waved it about.

He shook his head no.

"It's a little jacket I made for Yam. Sometimes the spring nights get cool. So this way, as the night wears on, you just slip it over his front legs. He'll be a much better actor if he doesn't get a chill."

"I'm afraid, Blanche, Yam's career is over."

"Why? What happened?"

"Oh, it has nothing to do with him. The production has been suspended."

"But I thought you said it went well."

"Yes, it was going well. But Doc Nightingale ran into a problem."

"On the set, you mean."

"Not on the set. In a motel. She shot a fella."

"Oh, Lord."

"Yep. Put two holes in him. So she doesn't have any time right now for a TV series."

"Well, then, maybe it's all for the best, Charlie. I wouldn't want Yam around violent people."

"True," he agreed. "Wouldn't want any harm to come to our Yam." The cat strolled past them and into his own room.

"He must be so tired," Blanche mused.

"Right. It was probably the most exhausting day of his life. You wouldn't believe how hard he worked."

"You're a fine and loving man, Charles Gravis."

"Well, that about does it for me, Blanche. So long." He stood, received her good-bye kiss, and walked out into the fresh air.

Trent Tucker turned to him the moment he climbed into the passenger seat. "By the way, Charlie, I forgot to ask you. When you transport Wyatt Earp around, are his six-guns in the carrier, too?"

A week had passed. Dr. Nightingale was in the throes of the second passionate love affair of her young life. The first, with the Philadelphia professor, had ended disastrously. But this one, she believed, would not turn out that way. And she really wasn't thinking of endings. She was happy. She was alive. She was working. And she was in love with Allie Voegler.

They met that evening in the bar just off Route 44. Allie sat on the bar stool and sipped a beer. She stood just next to him, her hand draped lightly over his shoulder. She had an apple juice in front of her.

Allie whispered close to her ear. "You've got me spinning . . . spinning . . . spinning. Chung says they ought to lift my driver's license. He says I'm in a daze."

Didi murmured back. "Maybe you have an undiagnosed inner ear problem. It's common in whitetail bucks this time of year."

Allie laughed. Didi kissed him.

Suddenly they heard a voice ring out: "Rye whiskey!"

It was the poet Burt Conyers, standing at the bar not more than five feet from them, resplendent in his sheepskin vest, sneakers, and bamboo cane. He looked wilder than ever.

The bartender addressed him warily. "I hope you got money to pay for it this time."

Conyers repeated his order and added, "And a small beer with it."

"Show me the money," the bartender said gently.

The old poet cursed, dug into his vest pocket and flung a mixture of dollar bills and coins onto the bar. One of the quarters rolled off onto the floor.

The drinks were set down in front of him. Conyers downed the shot in one gulp and the beer in two.

Then he walked over to the happy couple, standing about two feet back from the bar and tapping his cane on the linoleum.

"I want to declare something to you people," he announced.

"Declare whatever the hell you want," said Allie, obviously not happy at the interruption.

"I want to declare that not a single day has gone by that I have not loathed myself for what Ida and I did to those dogs. Not a single day, not a single hour, not a single minute. It's all over now. All the murders are over. All the murderers have been dealt with. So I can say it now. What I did was beyond comprehension. But we felt unable to strike at him directly. It was only the wretched creatures that could be reached. Poor Ida. She never wanted that to happen. It was I. Do you understand? It was I who moved the hives and baited them with the meat."

He stopped speaking for a minute and then laughed. It was a terrible sound brimming over with pain.

"Look who I've confessed to," he said.

He pointed a finger at Allie. "You sent an innocent man to prison, and to his death.

"And you"—he was now pointing at Didi—"the noble lady of veterinary medicine—you put two bullets in a fleeing man's back."

He turned and began to walk out of the bar. But Allie called him back. "Have a drink on me." Allie had been wounded by the old poet's words, wounded all over again, but the only thing he could think to do was offer Burt another drink. Perhaps it would help him forget a little. If nothing else, it might help him to sleep. Allie understood what sleepless nights were all about.

"I can drink no more. I have to watch my liver. A Promethean punishment is waiting for me in hell. I will be chained to a rock and my liver will continually be devoured by fox-hounds. A just punishment. My liver must remain intact."

He laughed again, this time even more bitterly. Then he came close to Didi. "I just came from Ida's grave," he said. "I placed the last bouquet on it. She'll know now, all the bills have been paid. Or maybe she won't know. Poor Ida was cremated. I scattered her ashes there. She is dust. The ashes may have blown all the way to Albany by now, for all we know."

"Burt, have a drink," Allie persisted. "And read us one of your poems."

Burt Conyers shook his head and walked out.

"That is one difficult man," the bartender said. "How about a refill for you folks?"

"Play some music, Allie," Didi asked, her voice low. "Play some Patsy Cline for me."

He took the quarters from the bar and walked over to the jukebox.

It had been a long day. Dr. Nightingale suddenly felt weary. But she also felt loved.

Turn the page to preview the next
Dr. Nightingale mystery:

DR. NIGHTINGALE
MEETS PUSS 'N' BOOTS

Coming from Signet in August 1997

The taxi was right on time. Eight a.m. exactly. Deirdre Quinn Nightingale, DVM, looked through the living room curtain and rolled her eyes heavenward. Along with the four family retainers that she referred to as her elves—who worked for her in return for their room and board—she was headed for a week's vacation in New York City.

The cab would take them to the train station in Poughkeepsie, where they would board the 8:45 for Grand Central Station. Didi had been hoping against hope that something might delay the arrival of the taxi. But it was no good. The driver was opening the trunk now, and her four traveling companions were loading it up with their luggage. The young vet sighed deeply, grabbed her little valise, and went out to join the party.

On the train, the group chattered excitedly about the trip—except for Didi, that is, who was hardly in a party mood. In fact, she was downright glum. But she had good reason to be glum. This was a forced vacation as far as she was concerned. She hadn't wanted to go anywhere at all, and she definitely had no desire to spend a week in Manhattan in the August heat in the company of her elves.

The circumstances that brought this little jaunt into being had been decidedly strange. One week earlier, the United Villages Fair had taken place. It was a two-day event, just outside Hillsbrook, that tried to mimic the massive week-long bacchanal called the Dutchess County Fair, which always occurred around Labor Day.

Didi had served as judge in several of the contests, such as Best Calf and Best Working Dog. All the elves had been in attendance as well.

Mrs. Tunney, Didi's housekeeper, had been one of the judges in the pie baking contest. Didi found this inexplicable, since Mrs. Tunney herself never baked pies. Charlie Gravis, Didi's geriatric veterinary assistant, had helped out at one of the "pitch and toss" booths. Trent Tucker, the so-called handyman, had hired on as a garbage removal man.

And Abigail, as usual, had just wandered about.

On the second and last day of the fair there was the traditional talent contest. A portable stage was set up and a prize announced. The stage and mike were "open"—anyone could walk up and perform. And they did. There were jugglers, dancers, psychics, yodelers, magicians. There were local rock bands, violinists, and a woman who played "Unforgettable" on old wooden birdcages.

There was even a dog trainer with five Afghan hounds who leaped over one another and then through burning hoops.

And then, to everyone's astonishment, up walked Abigail.

Now, people in Hillsbrook knew that Abigail was one of Dr. Nightingale's elves. They also knew that this thin, very fair, and ethereal-looking young woman of twenty-four years was, as someone had once described her, three bales short of a full hayloft.

They knew some other things about Abigail: that she was vaguely related to either Trent Tucker or Mrs. Tunney; that while she rarely spoke, she did sing in the church choir; and that from time to time she burst out of her shell and into some very outrageous behavior.

But what she did when she walked up on the stage was not outrageous at all.

Abigail simply began to sing—a capella. She sang three songs that Joan Baez had sung in her early days: "Black Is the Color," "Railroad Bill," and "Blue, You Good Dog You."

Abigail had mesmerized the crowd. And one of the enchanted listeners was a visiting Manhattanite named Carl Schirra, who owned one of those country western bars—Boots—in the section of New York City known as Chelsea.

Schirra said that folk singers were making a big comeback . . . that Abigail was a budding star . . . that he was going to book her into Boots for a week . . . that he'd pay all hotel expenses for her and her family in New York City (not a fancy hotel, mind you, but a clean one) . . . that she had to make up her mind now . . . that this was the chance of a lifetime.

Abigail accepted the offer and announced the news to her "family"—Charlie, Trent, and Mrs. Tunney. The elves jumped at the invitation, but before the day was out they were begging Didi to accompany them. Not least of all because they were frightened of the big bad apple and Didi was wise to the ways of the city. She had spent several years in vet school in Philadelphia, and that was practically the same thing as being born a city girl, wasn't it?

Didi bent to the pressure. But there was another factor contributing to her decision to make the trip. One of Didi's vet school classmates, Ilona Baer, had opened what had become a very successful small animal practice in the city. Ilona had been asking Didi to visit for years. Didi had postponed the visit time and

again. Now she decided that she might as well
stun two birds with one stone. Ilona was ecstatic when Didi telephoned to say that she would
spend the week with her while the elves stayed
at the hotel.

Didi did have a professional reason for visiting Ilona. A week or so with one of the premier
young veterinarians in New York would give
her some intensive hands-on experience with
diseases of and surgery on cats. Didi was quite
happy with her large animal practice in Hillsbrook, but she had always been fascinated with
felines and wanted to know more about them.

And there was another enticement. Ilona had
developed a passion for cold climes and was always going off on adventures at the North or
South Pole, where she studied ecological niches.
It was really just a hobby, but she had become
so knowledgeable that the Central Park Zoo
used her as a part-time nutritional consultant
for the polar bears, sea lions, and penguins. The
thought that her old school chum was dealing
with Gus, the now world-famous neurotic polar
bear who had required psychiatric help, was
simply delicious.

The quintet, spread out over three rows of
seats on the dreary Amtrak car, was an odd
mix. The sixtyish Mrs. Tunney was dressed for
a summer church wedding, including a flamboyant hat.

Charlie Gravis wore the vest to a long-forgotten Sunday best dress suit over a white T-shirt that was two sizes too big for his small frame.

Only a year younger than Abigail, Trent Tucker was wearing snug-fitting black jeans and a faded black denim shirt. He had heard that hip people in Manhattan always wore black.

Abigail, the budding heir to Joan Baez's throne, wore her usual shapeless long blue dress. Blue was her favorite color, and she seemed to have a homemade frock in every shade of that color.

As for Didi, she was dressed just as she might be dressed to go out on rounds—denims, washed-out sweatshirt, and rain sneakers. Her only concession to the occasion was the addition of tiny black pearl earrings.

Since Didi was wiry in build and her black hair was cut short, it was entirely possible that someone viewing the entourage would think that here was a set of grandparents taking their three just-out-of-college grandchildren to New York as a graduation present.

Ten minutes outside New York City, the train slowed and then came to a stop. The air conditioning and the car lights went out. Even though it was still morning, the atmosphere in the car very quickly became stifling.

"I knew we should have taken an earlier train," Mrs. Tunney whined.

"What's our rush?" Charlie replied. "We don't have to be at that nightclub till six in the evening. Abigail doesn't start singing till seven."

"What about Miss Quinn? What about all her appointments?" Mrs. Tunney kept on.

Didi didn't respond. She had told Mrs. Tunney a half dozen times that she had no appointments at all . . . that she would spend the whole day with them . . . and she would leave for her friend Ilona's place after Abigail's debut.

In fact, the only thing that wasn't planned was whether to leave after Abigail's first or second performance. She was scheduled to perform two sets—one at seven and one at nine. Another singer was to perform at eight and again at ten. And then the headliner for the night—a zydeco band—was to go on at eleven.

"We won't be here long," Charlie said reassuringly, staring out the window to assess the situation. He spoke with supreme authority, as if he were an old hand at such things, a veteran railroad man.

The train sat immobile for one hour and nineteen minutes. It pulled into Grand Central terminal two hours late.

The hotel that Carl Schirra had selected for them was called the Kenmare. It was only three blocks away from the station and was one of those new "all suite" places that provide multi-room accommodations at reasonable prices, and virtually no service. It had been converted from a welfare hotel.

They took their own bags up to the third floor and entered a rather nice complex of rooms: a large living room, two small bedrooms, a tiny kitchen, and a bathroom. The suite was heavily air conditioned—actually cold.

Everyone washed up and changed. They all seemed happy that, the stalled train aside, there had been no major disasters. They rested for an hour, then walked to Thirty-fourth Street and ate hugely at a fast-food Italian place called Sbarro's. Their next stop was Macy's.

Sometime during their spree at the world's largest store they lost both Abigail and Charlie Gravis. It wasn't until 3:20 that store security located Abigail, who was standing on the corner of Thirty-fifth and Seventh Avenue, across the street from the store. At 3:45 they found Charlie fast asleep in a lounger in the furniture department.

Worse than that, Trent Tucker had spent his entire cash reserve on a pair of Elvis-type boots.

"It could have been worse," Didi reminded her troops—and herself—after they landed back in the hotel with all the packages and all the bodies.

The problem was that it was now almost five and Schirra had told them to be at Boots by six. "We have fifteen minutes to dress," Didi announced.

Chaos ensued, but the task got done. They were ready for dear Abigail's leap from obscurity to America's most beloved warbler.

A cab transported them to Tenth Avenue and Twenty-second Street. "I love this city!" Trent Tucker declared to the Nigerian driver as he exited. It was Didi who paid the fare.

As they approached Boots, Mrs. Tunney stopped in her tracks. She had halted so suddenly that she tripped up Abigail.

Charlie helped the folksinger regain her feet. He barked at the old housekeeper. "What's the matter with you, woman?"

Now pale, she answered, "I just had the terrible feeling that something is going to go wrong up in Hillsbrook."

"Stop worrying. Everything is covered," Didi said in her professional soother's manner. And indeed, everything was. Didi's best friend, Rose Vigdor, had volunteered to look after the yard dogs, the hogs, and the horse. As for the Nightingale veterinary practice, two local vets were covering that.

The entourage proceeded.

"Where's Abigail's name at?" Trent Tucker

demanded when they reached the front door of the club.

There was no marquee, no poster or announcement of anyone except the headlining zydeco band: the Bayou Blasters. And even the flyer announcing them had been done on the cheap—a plain white piece of photocopy copy with the words TONIGHT! THE BAYOU BLASTERS lettered in red magic marker and thumbtacked to a board next to the entrance.

Once the group was inside the club, Didi realized that Boots was not what she had expected. It wasn't even close to what she'd expected.

There was a long, narrow bar up front. Past that the space grew wide enough to accommodate about fifteen small tables with four chairs placed around each.

A raised wooden stage was nestled along the back wall so that bar patrons as well as the customers at the tables could see and hear the show.

On the stage was a standing microphone, a full set of drums, and some sound equipment. The walls were covered with reproductions of Wild West era "Wanted" posters. Particularly variations of the William Bonney—alias Billy the Kid—posters.

"Are you the people from Hillsbrook?" asked the petite lady bartender.

"Four from Hillsbrook, one from the moon," quipped Charlie Gravis, pointing at Trent

Tucker, who had obviously fallen instanta-neously in love with the young woman.

"I'm Arden," she said. She came out and led the contingent to a table, pulling up two extra chairs.

Carl Schirra then popped up out of nowhere and greeted them all extravagantly. As if Abi-gail were Streisand and the others her retinue.

Arden left and came back with five bottles of Sierra Nevada Pale Ale, five tall glasses, and two big bowls of popcorn. She poured the ale for them under Mrs. Tunney's baleful gaze.

Suddenly, Mrs. Tunney screamed.

A large gray Persian cat had appeared from nowhere, jumped up, and was now draped across her lap. The cat's long tail was swishing happily.

Arden came to the rescue of the startled Mrs. Tunney. She pulled the cat off the beleaguered housekeeper and held him up admiringly. "It's just his way of being friendly. This is Molson. He lives here. He's been a bit under the weather, but he seems to be fine now."

Then she let Molson down, and the big cat wandered off.

Didi watched him move. Mrs. Tunney apolo-gized for her fright. "It's not that I don't like cats," she explained. "It's just that it was so sudden and he's so . . . big."

"Yes," Charlie Gravis said, "he sure is big. I like big cats and little women."

Trent Tucker laughed. Mrs. Tunney gave Charlie a look informing him she didn't think his comment was funny.

Schirra, who was a darkly handsome middle-aged man with a bushy mustache and friendly eyes, leaned over and kissed Abigail's cheek. "You're on in thirty-five minutes. I'll intro you."

Then he was gone. Didi looked around the place. It was empty; not one other patron had come in. Oh, well, she thought, there was still time for an audience to gather.

For a moment, sitting there with her elves, Doctor Nightingale felt very good—a kind of warm déja vu had come upon her. It was as if she were back in school in Philadelphia, and she and her chums had gone to a funky bar in South Philly to relax and celebrate after exams.

That feeling evaporated when a tipsy middle-aged man entered the room and worked his way back to a table. He looked quite lost.

Then another table was occupied by two women wearing flamboyant print summer dresses and drinking Bloody Mary's. They looked like school teachers from the Midwest on a binge.

The audience was completed when a well-dressed young man came in, sat at a front table, and immediately began working on the *New York Times* crossword puzzle.

Well, Didi thought, it probably gets crowded later on. It probably will be packed for Abigail's second set, at nine. And it will probably be a very young crowd—with nary a single middle-aged lush.

Trent Tucker ordered five more ales even though neither Mrs. Tunney nor Abigail nor Didi had touched hers. "Who's paying for this?" Charlie demanded.

"Who cares?" Trent retorted, shrugging his shoulders.

Didi began to watch Abigail for signs of anxiety or anticipation. There seemed to be none. Abigail just sat quietly, her eye on a nearby Wanted poster. The outfit she had chosen to perform in was one of Didi's mother's old dresses, a loose white cotton one with maroon stitching at the sleeves and neck, along with white flat-heeled sandals.

Mr. Schirra reappeared. This time he was wearing a blue blazer with a red bow tie. He walked to the wall beside the stage and flicked a switch. The bar lights dimmed and the stage lights went on.

He climbed the stage and fiddled with the mike—using the standard *one two three* testing script—until he got it adjusted.

"Ladies and gentlemen, welcome to Boots. It

is not often that a club owner like myself has the good luck of discovering an awesome new talent. I am not a man who trades in superlatives, so when I say awesome, I mean—"

"Hey!"

The shout had come from the bar area, bringing Schirra's introduction to a halt. The audience and Schirra himself all looked back at what was apparently a bike messenger, a chunky young blond woman sporting a helmet and tight-fitting lycra cycling pants. Arden, the pretty bartender, tried to silence the girl, but to no avail.

"Where do you want these?" the messenger yelled to Schirra and held up a bouquet of cut flowers. "And I need a signature," she added testily.

"What the hell is the matter with you?" Schirra shouted back angrily. "Can't you see there's a performance going on here? You deliver flowers *after* a performance, you nitwit."

He then glared down at the Hillsbrook table, as if to imply they had to have been responsible for the transgression.

The messenger shrugged and began walking boldly toward the stage. She dumped the bedraggled bouquet of white roses wrapped in blue tissue onto the stage, right at the club owner's feet, and then she waved the receipt in front of the steaming Schirra's nose.

"All right, all right! If it'll make you get out of

here, I'll sign. But I don't have a goddamn pencil," he said gruffly.

"Anything to oblige," she answered sarcastically, reaching into her worn bag.

But that was no pencil in her hand. She had pulled out a small derringer. And now she was using it to shoot Carl Schirra in the face. Twice.

The girl ran lightly out of the club as the dying man fell off the stage and onto the lap of the young man with the newspaper, splattering him and his crossword with blood.

The audience—what there was of it—went wild with panic. Everyone screaming . . . diving for safety beneath the tables . . . crying.

Schirra had managed to entwine one of the many long cords on the stage around his leg as he fell. The microphone wobbled a few times and hit the wooden floor with the most horrible scream of all.

Didi lay on the floor. She had bruised the heels of her palms while diving for cover. Everything was quiet now. Everything and everyone was still.

Then Didi heard a rasping sound. At first she thought Carl Schirra was still alive.

But then she saw that the sound was coming from Molson. The big gray cat was scratching his back on one of the dead man's shoes.

DR. NIGHTINGALE COMES HOME

Deirdre "Didi" Quinn Nightingale needs to solve a baffling mystery to save her struggling veterinary practice in New York state. Bouncing in her red jeep along country roads, she is headed for a herd of beautiful, but suddenly very crazy, French Alpine dairy goats of a "new money" gentleman farmer. Diagnosing the goats' strange malady will test her investigative skills and win her a much needed wealthy client. But the goat enigma is just a warm-up for murder. Old Dick Obey, her dearest friend since she opened her office, is found dead, mutilated by wild dogs. Or so the local police force says. Didi's look at the evidence from a vet's perspective convinces her the killer species isn't canine but human. Now she's snooping among the region's forgotten farms and tiny hamlets, where a pretty sleuth had better tread carefully on a twisted trail of animal tracks, human lies, and passions gone deadly. . . .

DR. NIGHTINGALE
RIDES THE ELEPHANT

Excitement is making Deirdre "Didi" Nightingale, DVM, feel like a child again. There'll be no sick cows today. No clinic. No rounds. She is going to the circus. But shortly after she becomes veterinarian on call for a small traveling circus, Dolly, an extremely gentle Asian elephant, goes berserk and kills a beautiful dancer before a horrified crowd. Branded a rogue, Dolly seems doomed, and in Didi's opinion it's a bum rap that shouldn't happen to a dog. Didi is certain someone tampered with the elephant and is determined to save the magnificent beast from being put down. Her investigation into the tragedy leads her to another corpse, an explosively angry tiger trainer, and a "little people" performer with a big clue. Now, in the exotic world of the Big Top, Didi is walking the high wire between danger and compassion . . . knowing that the wild things are really found in the darkness, deep in a killer's twisted mind.

DR. NIGHTINGALE
GOES TO THE DOGS

Veterinarian Deirdre "Didi" Quinn Nightingale has the birthday blues. It's her day, and it's been a disaster. First she's knee-deep in mud during a "bedside" visit to a stud pig. Then she's over her head in murder when she finds ninety-year-old Mary Hyndman shot to death at her rural upstate farm.

The discovery leaves Deirdre bone-weary and still facing Mary's last request: to deliver a donation to Alsatian House, a Hudson River monastery famous for its German shepherds. Deirdre finds the retreat filled with happy dogs, smiling monks, and peace.

This spur-of-the moment vacation rejuvenates Deirdre's flogging strength and spirit until another murder tugs on her new leash on life. Deirdre's investigative skills tell her this death is linked to Mary's. But getting her teeth into this case may prove too tough for even a dauntless DVM . . . when a killer with feral instincts brings her a hair's breadth from death.

DR. NIGHTINGALE
GOES THE DISTANCE

Intending to forget about her sick cats and ailing cows for one night, Deirdre "Didi" Quinn Nightingale, DVM, is all dressed up for a champagne-sipping pre-race gala at a posh thoroughbred farm. She never expects death to be on the guest list while hobnobbing with the horsey set and waiting to meet the famous equine vet Sam Hull. But when two shots ring out, two bodies lie in the stall of the year's most promising filly.

The renowned Dr. Hull is beyond help, and the filly's distraught owner offers Didi a fee and a thoroughbred all her own to find this killer. Now Deirdre is off snooping in a world of bloodlines, blood money, and bloody schemes. The odds are against this spunky vet who may find that her heart's desire is at stake—and murder waiting at the finish line. . . .

DR. NIGHTINGALE
ENTERS THE BEAR CAVE

Veterinarian Deirdre "Didi" Nightingale is happily taking a break from her practice to join a research team tagging pregnant black bears in the northern Catskills. Awaiting her are the thrill of adventure, the fun of taking her friend Rose along—and murder.

No sooner do she and Rose arrive at the base camp than they run into the bullet-riddled body of the caretaker. Although local police insist the murder has nothing to do with the scientific expedition, Deirdre feels something fishy is afoot in bear country. She soon finds the paw print of a monster-size bruin, a creature that is a Catskill legend—and a growing reason to suspect one of her group is a killer. Meanwhile, the woods are lovely, dark, and deep. And, for a vet on the trail of a murderer, most deadly.